DIRT LINE

DIRT LINE

DWARVISH DIRTY DOZEN™ SERIES BOOK TWO

AARON D. SCHNEIDER
MICHAEL ANDERLE

DISRUPTIVE IMAGINATION

This book is a work of fiction. All of the characters, organizations, and events portrayed in this novel are either products of the author's imagination or are used fictitiously. Sometimes both.

Copyright © 2022 LMBPN Publishing
Cover Art by Jake @ J Caleb Design
http://jcalebdesign.com / jcalebdesign@gmail.com
Cover copyright © LMBPN Publishing
A Michael Anderle Production

LMBPN Publishing supports the right to free expression and the value of copyright. The purpose of copyright is to encourage writers and artists to produce the creative works that enrich our culture.

The distribution of this book without permission is a theft of the author's intellectual property. If you would like permission to use material from the book (other than for review purposes), please contact support@lmbpn.com. Thank you for your support of the author's rights.

LMBPN Publishing
PMB 196, 2540 South Maryland Pkwy
Las Vegas, NV 89109

Version 1.00, August 2022
ebook ISBN: 979-8-88541-722-8
Paperback ISBN: 979-8-88541-723-5

THE DIRT LINE TEAM

Thanks to our JIT Team:

Peter Manis
Zacc Pelter
John Ashmore
Kelly O'Donnell
Paul Westman
Diane L. Smith
Dorothy Lloyd

If we've missed anyone, please let us know!

Editor
SkyFyre Editing Team

DEDICATIONS

This book is dedicated to those who aren't afraid to draw lines in the sand. In a world that seems more and more in love with uncertainty and what amounts to no more than moral cowardice I appreciate those who will plant their feet and declare, "This far and no farther." You may not always be right, and it often may not seem like it matters, but to those of us growing weary in a dark and shapeless world, it is heartening to find those willing to stand for something.

Here's to you, my brothers and sisters. May your feet find solid ground on which to stand.

— Aaron

To Family, Friends and
Those Who Love
to Read.
May We All Enjoy Grace
to Live the Life We Are
Called.

— Michael

ACKNOWLEDGMENTS

I'd like to acknowledge that this book and indeed a good share of my career as an author is because of great people who were willing to take a chance on me, even when there were times it seemed the investment would never pay off. To my parents, teachers, my wife, and of course, my publishers. Without your willingness to take a risk on me, I know I wouldn't be able to do what I do.

It didn't always pan out, and I'm sure I have incurred some debts I'll never be able to repay, but I wanted you to know I see you, and I appreciate all that you've done. God bless.

— Aaron

I was born one morning, it was drizzlin' rain
Fightin' and trouble are my middle name

— *16 Tons*, Tennessee Ernie Ford

For my unconquerable soul.

In the fell clutch of circumstance
I have not winced nor cried aloud.

—Invictus, William Ernest Henley

When midnight mists are creeping,
And all the land is sleeping,
Around me tread the mighty dead,
And slowly pass away.
Lo, warriors, saints, and sages,
From out the vanished ages,
With solemn pace and reverend face
Appear and pass away.
The blaze of noonday splendour,
The twilight soft and tender,
May charm the eye: yet they shall die,
Shall die and pass away.
But here, in Dreamland's centre,

> No spoiler's hand may enter,
> These visions fair, this radiance rare,
> Shall never pass away.
> I see the shadows falling,
> The forms of old recalling;
> Around me tread the mighty dead,
> And slowly pass away.

—Dreamland, Charles Lutwidge Dodgson

SOUTHERN YSGAND VALE MAP

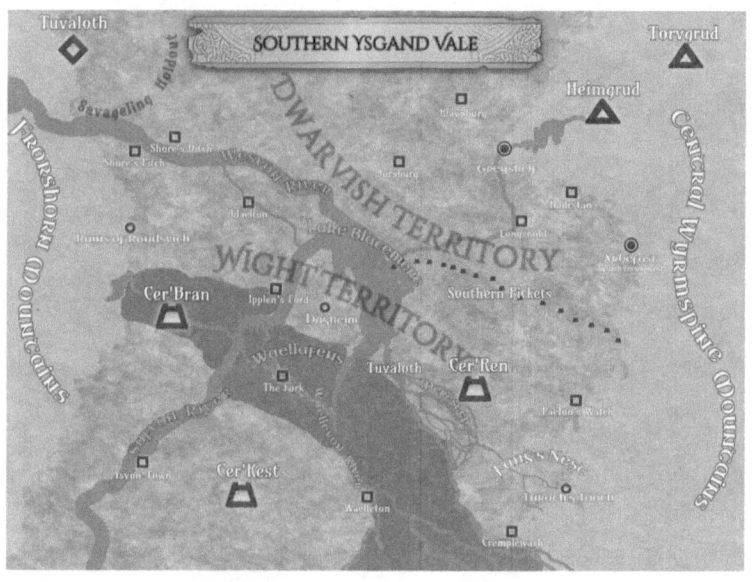

LEXICON

Military Ranks

— Enlisted —

Dwan - The base rank of the Holt'Dwan and also a term that generally refers to a dwarf serving as a soldier

Fordwan - A line officer, typically promoted from veteran dwan

Ascedwan - A dwarf soldier who has developed a useful skill (cooking, herbology, engineering, musical instrument, etc.), marking them out for additional pay/responsibility

— Commissioned Officer —

Schildwan - quartermaster of a division
Tweldwan - commander of a division
— Command Staff —
Kuadwan - command staff, responsible for logistical matters
Lardwan - command staff, responsible for communication and intelligence

Vindwan - command staff, responsible for tactical direction

Ondwan - command staff, supreme commander of the Holt'Dwan

— Informal Positions —

Cubldwan - An unofficial position, represents when a soldier is selected to work under a superior officer, usually either a tweldwan or one of the command staff

Military Terminology

Adyrclaf - a class of theropod typically used as a mount by the svartalf

Blotferow - a class of trained and specially bred pigs that is suitable for use in battle

Duabuw - standard-issue crossbow of the dwarven army

Holt'Dwan - A dwarven army, typically composed of between 8 to 12 divisions

Magsax - standard-issue sword of the dwarven army

Worcsvine - a class of trained and specially bred pigs that are suitable for draft work

Slurs

Badger - Derived from drawing a comparison between the animals and dwarfs

Clacker/Creaker/Rattler/Shuffler - slur for the ambulatory undead who serve in the wight army. Given for the sounds they make

Grem - Derived from drawing comparisons between mythical gremlins and goblins

Longshanks - Can be used for any people group taller than dwarfs, but typically used for humans

Myrkling - Derived from the Dwarvish word for dark/dangerous forest (myrkvaul) and denotes an elf of svartalf or dark elf lineage

Savageling - slur for the wosealf or wild elves of the Ysgand Vale

Wheezer - slur for a wight after the sound of the undead voices

PROLOGUE

"This can't be right."

Waelon scowled but refused to look up from the shot he was sighting even as the young dwarfess buzzed in his ear. He expected witchery had addled her brains with elvish ideas of the world, so she was the last one to bring on this sort of expedition. Yet, Torbjorn had insisted upon it.

Just above his sighting peg, the she-bear he was aiming at chuffed and pawed at the earth, raising her head to sniff the air.

"Has to be done," he rasped, adjusting the sighting peg with a slight twist. "If you're going to blame someone, blame Gromic. That tub never could keep a tidy camp."

The bear swiped at the ground, claws raking through the cover of earth and forest detritus. Neither dwarf could see the camp scraps Waelon had deposited in a shallow divot in the earth, but there was no doubt the bear did.

"That's not what I'm talking about," Tomza said, her breath coiling on the frosty air. "She wouldn't be staying up here instead of going to the valley unless she had a den."

Waelon was about to growl at her to be quiet, but the sounds from the bear stopped, and both froze. Hardly daring to breathe, they waited and watched the bear's dark eyes roving over where they crouched downwind. Waelon had picked his spot well, and he was confident that even if she barreled down on them, he could put a bolt, maybe two, into her.

He'd have preferred to be on the solid stone overlook or, barring that, up a tree, but that hadn't been an option. The only trees at this altitude were springy, scraggly things a goblin would be hard-pressed to nest in.

"Look at her," Waelon said softly. "Her coat's hangin' slack, and the old girl is rangy. If she bedded down now, she wouldn't last through winter."

The former ranger could feel the intensity of Tomza's eyes boring into the side of his head.

"Exactly," she declared a touch too loud. "If she is so thin, why stay up here where winter is coming early unless something is keeping her from going down?"

Waelon felt something tickling the back of his mind, telling him the lass was onto something. With a curse, he lowered his weapon and looked at her.

"What if she's stayin' here because she's got cubs in that den?" he challenged, his peripheral vision still registering the hunched form of the bear.

"She's not liable to leave them there even if she is hungry. Those cubs would need just as much fattening."

"So, what are you say—"

The former ranger's words cut off as an ursine rumble rolled like thunder.

Waelon's eyes snapped forward, but the bear's threat was not directed toward them. Leaving her claw-raked samples, her snout swung to a line of figures materializing from the chill mist creeping between the scrubby trees. She chomped at the air with teeth as the figures advanced, their movements unhurried. There was no fear, no urgency, no caution… No life.

"Kak," Waelon hissed. He shouldered his duabuw and began to slowly creep back. "Come on."

Tomza gaped as the figures resolved from dark silhouettes to the tall, ragged figures that had haunted her sleep. They'd once been soldiers, the uniformity of their tattered and crumbling armor and arms serving as testament. The spears of corroded bronze in their bony hands rose in unison as their bodies answered to wills stripped of fear, doubt, or care. The pale shine of their eyes was a cold and alien light like stars.

That light pierced her as though all were turning toward her, impassive and merciless. Memory made her nostrils fill with smoke and her ears with the sounds of dying.

Tomza started as a rough hand seized her shoulder, and for an instant, she was certain she was being hauled around to face a looming figure with a bronze spear raised high. Instead, it was a scowling dwarf with cheeks as red as his blazing beard.

"Damn it, lass," Waelon rasped in a hoarse whisper. "Move yer arse!"

She blinked twice, then with a slack-jawed nod, made to follow him.

Down below, the she-bear's growls became groans. Her dark gaze swung from side to side, nose drinking in the smell of death. On they came, confounding her instincts as she settled on a single desperate stratagem: *charge*.

Tomza heard the ursine's final roaring rush and looked back to see the towering figures plunge their spears through sagging hide and bunching sinew. The bear's momentum was enough to carry her onto the impaling rods, and the seemingly implacable line bowed under her fury. Bony feet in peeling sandals gouged troughs in the ground in the final moments of hope for the bear.

Tomza knew the servants of the wights struck down hope wherever it sprang up. They had purged the lower Vale of dwarfs just for being in their way, and they now extinguished the bear because she'd had the temerity to stand before them.

The bear's struggling faltered, then, with an audible creak of sinew and a rustle of scale armor, the undead heaved the beast to one side. A final low, rattling groan faded to silence as an unliving foot tramped over her corpse.

Biting her lip to keep from crying out, Tomza returned her attention to scrambling with Waelon across the slope. Her breath came in ragged gulps that tasted of blood. They dared not look back until they got to a ridge that provided an unimpaired view of the mountainside.

Though elevation made them less threatening, there was no mistaking how eerie the undead looked as they advanced up the slope with measured steps.

"They're coming for us," Tomza said, her throat tightening. She hated how frightened her voice sounded. "They've caught up, and they're going to corner us."

Waelon frowned at the advancing undead, sweeping his gaze left and right before looking up at the mountain's grim face.

"They're going to try," the big dwarf said. "But Stones know we're not going to make it easy. Come on. At the rate they're going, we can rouse the others."

Tomza sucked her lip as she peered over the edge of the shelf. She wanted to cry out and cast herself off in despair and defiance. Her nightmares, horrors no longer bound to the realms of memory and dreams, were coming, but she would not let them take her. This morbid solution to the encroaching enemy took her by surprise with its sudden and ferocious appearance, preventing her from following Waelon.

What was the point? Why keep up this fight? Her life had been fear and deprivation for so long. What was she still fighting for? Wouldn't it be easier to end it here and now? If she did it right, Waelon might think it was an accident, a fatigued misstep. Then her name wouldn't be maligned after her exit from this life.

Coward!

If the self-destructive thoughts had been a beast pouncing, the fiery repudiation in her soul was a volcano erupting. Bilious recriminations flooded her mind, and before she understood what was happening, her feet carried after Waelon. Her face burned with shame as well as exertion as she bounded up the slope.

Gutless coward! How dare you even think it!

Each thump of boot on stone drove the thoughts deeper into her mind until her soul howled inside her…or was that the wind keening over the mountainside? Was the rasping her fury gnawing at the inside of her skull or just the breath in her lungs burning as cold air rushed in and out? Did she care as long as it all propelled her far from those things and that ledge where terror had nearly plucked her away forever? Or was this just cowardice in a different form?

"We need to get the others up and moving," Waelon said. "With any luck, we can put enough distance between us and them to see us clear before the clackers know we're here."

Well, that answered Tomza's questions.

On they scrambled until they came to another ledge. They paused for a moment to see below them the chill mist hanging about the slope, creating a concealing veil.

"They could… right below…we'd never know," the dwarfess panted, every other word swallowed by another hungry gulp of air.

"Aye," Waelon agreed. "But we'd hear 'em. One good thing about fighting the rotters. You can almost always hear 'em coming."

Tomza made time in her gasping to turn an incredulous eye on the dwarven ranger.

"Why didn't we hear them coming before?" she demanded.

Waelon scowled, his eyes flashing dangerously.

"Didn't help that I had you chewing my ear the whole time," he spat, then held up a hand for silence. "Quiet, I think I heard something."

Her mouth shut with an audible click, drawing another wilting glare from the big dwarf. The sound had hardly faded when he nodded grimly. Just beneath the breath of the wind was the sound of undead feet tromping, closer than they had any right to be.

The dead were coming.

Waelon's eyes swung around to assess the craggy landscape above them, then followed the line of the ridge to the narrow gully where the Bad Badgers had made camp. He nodded and seized Tomza by the arm, drawing her close enough to whisper into her ear, "Get to camp. Tell the others to move. I'll be right behind you."

Tomza's gaze had been fixed on the drifting mist below, but at the instructions, her attention swiveled to the older dwarf. She wanted to demand to know what he was planning, but the ranger's scowl kept her quiet. This was not the time for debate, and from his grim look, pressing the issue might be downright hazardous to her health.

Tomza nodded, and with a final hissed "Be careful," she set off along the ridge quickly and quietly.

She wanted to turn to see what he was doing, but she had a job. The ridge was wide enough that she could move along it comfortably. Frost had turned to ice that clung in jagged patches here and there. As surefooted as any other of her kind, she wouldn't fall off, but a stumble would make noise and draw attention to the camp when every second was vitally important.

She made it around the curve of the ridge to the mouth of the gully. Ober straightened from his lookout's perch on a boulder. Her brother raised the duabuw he'd leveled at her to his shoulder and hopped down. Tomza winced at every sound as she scuttled over scree and stone to reach him.

"What's going on?" Ober asked. "Where's Waelon?"

Tomza shushed him with a gesture, then leaned close.

"Clackers on the slope coming this way," she relayed, fighting to keep her voice steady. Ober tensed. "Waelon says to get everybody up and moving."

He nodded longer than was necessary, wrestling with his fear.

"Torbjorn and Utyrvaul aren't back yet," Ober whispered. "We can't leave without telling them what's up."

Tomza froze uncertainly. There was a grinding roar and both dwarfs looked around, expecting the rock above them to come crashing down.

Rising over the thunderous, tectonic bellow came a wild howl. *"I AM WAELON OF CLAN DAVISH, AND YOU CLACKERS CAN KISS MY ARSE!"*

The boom of something heavy crashing down the mountainside echoed. Ober turned on his heel and scuttled around the bend. Meanwhile, his sister raced back the way she had come, her boots skating more than once on the treacherous ice.

She came to within a half-dozen strides of the ledge where Waelon had first set her to her task and saw that the lip of rock was now a pile of stony debris. A few pebbles bounced to a stop as her eyes roved up to a vacant spot on the slope, like the gap of a missing tooth. She would never have noted the boulder that had once sat there, but like a missing incisor, its absence was glaringly obvious. The mists below had thinned in the wake of the miniature landslide.

Tomza's mind raced to catch up with her eyes, and her heart sank almost before her mind could form the thought.

He's gone.

Waelon's brash shout must have been uttered as he was carried away by the storm of displaced stone. His last defiance as he smote their pursuers and drew them away.

Tomza's legs wobbled, but she refused to let them give way. Allowing herself to be found by their pursuers would be a poor way to honor the dwarven ranger's sacrifice. It felt impossible to leave, though. She had no illusions that Waelon was not buried under a cairn of broken stone, as close to a burial as he would receive.

That couldn't be the end, could it? A life rudely but boldly lived couldn't just vanish without some token or gesture to commemorate it.

Eyes blurring with tears, she refused to let fall, she drew her stout magsax. A few strokes into the stone would have to do but at least it was something. Her old schildwan would have strangled her for abusing the steel so, but it seemed a small sin for so noble a cause.

Tomza turned as the mounded scree shifted. Her fist tightened around the hilt, her forlorn sniff becoming a ferocious snarl. Her terror of the undead thing trapped beneath the stone was gone, and her fury roared to life as she stalked forward.

"Oh, no, you don't," she growled, her voice feral and strange in her ears. "You won't cheapen it!"

A single arm burst from the rubble, and she lifted her blade for a hewing strike. She'd just begun to throw her weight behind the stroke when she saw the dwarvish runes tattooed across the knuckles. She nearly toppled over as she halted the weapon's swing.

As she scrambled to right herself, the lone arm flailed for purchase, raking at pebbles that slipped and scattered uselessly.

"Hold on," Tomza gasped. Her magsax tumbled to the ground as she pulled away the debris. Every sharp edge cut her hands, but she paid that no mind as she cast rock after rock behind her.

"Almost there," she panted, hoping against hope that she could be heard. "Just hold on. Almost there."

As though in answer, the groping hand found her shoulder and then her collar. It pulled with frightening strength, and she arched her back in resistance as she kept tearing at the rubble. Sweat ran down her face, and she swore through gritted teeth.

So close. Nearly there. So close...

The pile of stones shifted, and Waelon's head erupted. He

started coughing and spluttering. His hair and beard were caked with dirt and rock dust.

By his third gasp, he turned burning eyes on his savior.

"Stupid lass," he wheezed as Tomza freed more of his barrel chest with her efforts. "What are you doing? You're supposed to be—"

"Ober's getting them moving," she interrupted. "And you're welcome, you stubborn son of a—"

"Look out!" Waelon's freed arm shot out to drive her back with a hard shove.

A spike of rotten bronze drove between them and struck the rocks.

"Kak!" Tomza cried as she scuttled back. She groped in the debris, but her magsax evaded her bloody fingers.

The undead followed her movement, spear poised for a fatal thrust. She cried out in frustration and fear as her hand brushed her weapon's hilt, only to knock it away.

The end was coming.

The stab passed inches from Tomza's skull as she recoiled. The half-buried dwarf made a desperate grab at the long fleshless leg as her outstretched hand settled on a leather-wrapped hilt.

The undead's jaws clacked bone on bone—hence the name "clacker"—as it rounded on the nuisance clutching its leg. With a sound like tearing parchment, it tore its leg free of the dwarf's grip, leaving a peeling sheaf behind. Waelon snarled up at his foe, blood-laced spittle flying from his defiant lips.

"Come on, then! You forget how to kill a dwarf, you rotten whoreson?"

Cold light flared and the spear descended, only to miss again. Tomza rocketed into the undead like a cannonball. In the treacherous scree, the clacker found little purchase and toppled over.

The dwarfess fell with it to the ground, holding her broad-bladed sword in her upraised hand. Once, twice, thrice, the blade flashed down. With a final rustle, its armor went slack as gravel crunched beneath its crushed skull.

Chest heaving and eyes blazing, Tomza stomped over to Waelon. The red-bearded dwarf gave her a rare smile as he reached out.

"Just couldn't let me take all the credit, could you, lass?"

Tomza growled in answer and took his outstretched hand. It took a moment of grunting and cursing, but the big dwarf finally emerged, dribbling pebbles like a duck shedding raindrops.

With the magsax still in her hand, Tomza glared at the clacker's corpse.

"I hate those things," she rasped. "I hate them so much."

"They ain't natural, that's for sure," he puffed, stretching to make sure all his limbs were intact. The flesh of his arms showed layered bruises, but otherwise, he seemed to be fine.

"It's more than that," Tomza said. "It's because—"

Her confession was drowned out by the deep thunder of drums. They shared a frightened look as the slope below trembled beneath thousands of undead feet.

"Don't suppose we've got another mountainside to bury them with?" Tomza wheezed, fighting to force a smile onto her trembling lips.

"Don't suppose," Waelon grunted.

Tomza felt her stomach knot as they set off, thankful Waelon couldn't see her hands shivering as she struggled to sheath her sword.

CHAPTER ONE

"That doesn't bode well."

Torbjorn was already in motion, stout boots thumping in a counterrhythm to the damnable drums. He didn't bother speaking his thoughts on the subject.

Like the heartbeat of the earth, hard and heavy with its anger toward us and our failures. Klaus had always possessed a flair for the dramatic, and his descriptions of facing the first wight onslaught were no exception. When Torbjorn had been released from his cell in Graycliff, he'd had a chance to hear the deep thunder himself. He couldn't think of a better way to describe the experience. Now, every time he heard it, he recalled Klaus' words.

"Us and our failures," he growled to himself.

"What was that, Commander?" the svartalf called with a melodious lilt.

"Blade-eared bastard," the dwarf grumbled. The elf's long ears *did* serve a purpose. "Quit playing and catch up with the others."

In one leaping stride, the myrkling was level with Torbjorn, seeming to float over the rough ground.

"And abandon you to make it back alone?" Utyrvaul tittered. "Perish the thought."

"I'm not joking, you cheeky son of a...*ufh*," Torbjorn started. He'd been too busy watching the angle of the slope to notice the patch of ice in front of him. He tried to keep from skidding down the slope.

"See, look at you!" The svartling tutted as he extended a long-fingered hand. "What would they say if I arrived without you, and then you never trundled your way back?"

"They'd probably assume you looked after me like you did Lady Tegwylivere," the dwarf commander said, climbing to his feet. "Then Waelon would kill you."

Utyrvaul met the commander's eyes with a look of sincerest shock and dismay. Torbjorn could see something else slithering behind his eyes, though it was beyond the dwarf's ken.

"I don't know what you might mean by that, Commander," the myrkling intoned sadly. "But I can say that as much as I honored my Lady Bannerette, my regard and affection for you is exponentially greater."

Torbjorn endeavored to pay more attention to where he was putting his feet, but he spared a look at the enigmatic elf. If the elf was speaking, he was lying; that much the dwarf knew. However, the elf's continued assistance was of great value. His keen eyes had pierced the mists and seen the game track they'd used to stay ahead of the wights thus far. He also helped Torbjorn find a way to skirt the arm of the mountain and make a break for the Valley to the Southern Pickets. All this for those whom he owed nothing.

Most svartalfs in the valley were mercenaries hired by the holt'dwans to serve as auxiliaries, but they were fickle creatures at the best of times. With enemies bearing down on them, Torbjorn constantly expected to awake to find the elf had run off. What kept the slippery mercenary here, with the claws of the undead at their heels?

Locked in such thoughts as well as the business of moving over the craggy ground, Torbjorn had no time for further discussion. They made their way to rendezvous with the rest of the Bad Badgers. The constant sound of the drums did nothing to improve his spirit, but their droning pressure served as a potent incentive to keep going.

For a time, the world resolved into nothing but the next boulder to skirt or clamber over. His focus drowned out even the drums as Torbjorn sank into that narrow place where exertion was all-consuming. Muscles bunched and burned as he sought handholds and clear places to set his boots. Seconds and minutes melted into an eternity with no beginning and no end, only the next grip, the next step.

Staying within reach yet straining at the invisible leash like an eager hound, Utyrvaul danced over the stones. His presence at the periphery of the commander's vision was an annoyance but for the assurance that he was not alone or going astray. Like most dwarfs, Torbjorn kept his head in the labyrinthine rise, fall, and twist of the mountains. In the mist that was heavy about them, getting lost would be all too easy.

Torbjorn had just scrambled up and then slid down when he came to a rough stop beside Utyrvaul. The svartalf stood rigid, eyes narrowed to ruby slits as they pierced the fog with uncanny prescience.

"Most of them made it clear." He thrust his sharp chin toward what looked like a curtain of mist to Torbjorn. "It looks like the hunting party is lagging behind, and the undead have sent some skirmishers to harry them."

"Grem or menfolk?" Torbjorn asked, peering futilely through the fog. "How many?"

"Goblins," the svartalf replied. "Less than a dozen that I can see."

Torbjorn was torn between laughing and being indignant.

"That's it?" he growled as his gauntleted hand settled upon his magsax. "I don't know if I should be thankful or insulted."

"Neither," Utyrvaul replied.

A yowling shriek stood every hair on Torbjorn's arms to attention as he choked back a dismayed curse.

"I assume you know what that means," the svartalf said. "And what we must now do."

Torbjorn staved off the shudder that was creeping up his spine and met the elf's frown. Utyrvaul tried to shake his head, but he crumbled under Torbjorn's burning stare.

"Must we always engage in tiresome heroics?"

The commander thrust his chin toward the wall of fog, sweat-soaked beard hardly moving with the gesture.

"Find me a way down to them, and I'll do it myself."

Utyrvaul's frown deepened as his gaze swung back to the mist-swaddled mountainside. "Doubtful." He sighed, and one hand settled on the plundered sword at his belt. "But as I said, I've grown quite fond of you, Commander, and as you've said, I can't very well arrive at camp without you and keep my head. Let's just make this quick, shall we? Places to go, things to see, and all that."

"What was that sound?"

Tomza tried to twist as she supported Waelon with a shoulder under his arm. The dwarf seemed miraculously unharmed despite his escapades. It could be that the cost of his bravery was a little slow in catching up with him, though. They'd set off at a brisk pace to try to catch up with the others, but the big dwarf's breathing had become labored, and he'd kept clutching his side. Tomza thought he'd broken more than one rib riding the landslide down. Every jostle and bump of their rough trek drained the ranger's endurance.

"Just leave me, lass," the dwarf growled, his dusty face riven with tracks of sweat. "You need to get to the others."

"Shut up and keep moving," she snarled for the fourth time. She wasn't sure if it was a trick of the mountains' acoustics or a product of her desperate imagination, but she could've sworn the drums sounded farther away.

"We're pulling ahead," she told him, her foot skidding over a frosty rock. "Hard to keep formation in the mountains, so the clackers are stuck crawling."

Waelon shook his head. Each breath was more pained, but his eyes burned under his heavy brows.

"Don't...don't understand," he groaned between hissing breaths. "Hunters... That screaming... Grem..."

She frowned and tried to shake stinging drops from her eyes with a toss of her head.

"Didn't sound like any goblin I've ever heard," she said. Icy thoughts of Waelon's flagging coherence spurred her to drive forward with renewed vigor. "Stay with me, ranger. We're going to make it."

Waelon staggered forward another half-dozen steps, then his dragging boot caught a wedge of rock, and they both were thrown to their knees.

"Not...not grem," the big dwarf wheezed, clutching both sides. "Gre...gremalkin."

Tomza was already on her feet, struggling to drag Waelon back up.

"Come on, big fella. Shift yourself," she urged, hauling upward to no avail.

Between her and her compatriot's heavy breaths, she heard displaced stones skitter. Tomza's fatigued mind took half a second to process the sound before she released her hold on Waelon to unlimber her duabuw. Her trembling arms worked the lever mechanically as she turned to where she'd heard the sounds.

Nothing but stone and fog greeted her eyes.

"What in the name of the Stone is a gremalkin?" she asked.

She felt as much as heard the rush of air as a lithe body leapt overhead. Then a high, keening voice gave her the answer.

"Gremalkin is *death*!"

CHAPTER TWO

The duabuw sang its throaty song, and the bolt tore through the shadow that was plunging down on Tomza.

The screech became a wail, but the diving form didn't slow. It plowed into her, and the dwarfess had a brief impression of slavering fangs snapping a hair's width from her face as she toppled backward. Claws raked at the mail on her shoulders but found little purchase, then the creature's weight rolled onto her. Its sleek body slid off, then another set of claws flashed by. A trailing hook tore a thin line over her ear.

Tomza snarled and raised the duabuw to shield her face, but the attacker was already past her.

"Bastards," Waelon gasped, one hand dropping to the axe at his belt. The sudden movement wracked his body with pain. Grinding out curses between clenched teeth, he pitched forward and caught himself with one hand, keeping the other clamped to his side.

The fall had saved his life. A second shadow had detached from the craggy walls and leapt forward, dark claws extended. The creature sailed over his broad back and hit the ground heavily, trying to turn the unexpected landing into a roll. Its back was covered with a tangled dark pelt, so the creature looked like a hairy wheel rolling across the rough terrain.

As the second spoiled attack bounced past, Tomza forced herself to rise despite her lack of breath. A thin, whining cry slipped through her pinched lips as she tried to accommodate the shock. The immediate threat of death gave her a quickness that seemed impossible in her current state. Hands clamped tight to the crossbow, she jumped to her feet and met a third attacker who was coming for Waelon.

With no time to prime the duabuw and no breath to offer a cry of warning, Tomza could only bull forward, using her weapon as a club. When its brass stock connected with a mouth full of needle teeth, it was all Tomza could do to keep her feet. Pairs of claws, one at her chest and the other at her loins, tore at the web of metal links guarding her flesh. She slashed the duabuw forward again and again.

"Damn you!" she cried in a shrill wheeze. "Let. *GO!*"

The final rebuke was paired with a head-butt to the already mashed face of her attacker. The claws lost their terrible strength, and the creature collapsed at her feet.

For the first time, she saw what faced her. She immediately wished that the mist would reclaim the creature. The body was too long and muscular for a goblin and too thin for a dwarf. She thought it might be a monstrous feline, yet its limbs were too long, and its spine was too knotted. In other circumstances, the creature might be graceful and elegant, but crumpled at her feet, it gave the impression of having agility and strength without poise. Its mangled muzzle and broken, jagged fangs did little to help this impression, though the smashed visage was reshaping and healing before her eyes.

Tomza recoiled as training drove her arms to prime her weapon again. By the second pump of the lever, the matted hair was falling out in clumps. On the third pump, the thing's goblinoid features appeared.

"Oh, kak," she muttered, wishing she wasn't keenly aware of the similarities between the changes she was seeing and what she'd witnessed on her brother. The thing at her feet was indistinguishable from a nude goblin but for the halo of fur arrayed about its limp form.

"Spirit-ridden!" Tomza stomped viciously. "Damned skin-changers."

The goblin's corpse shuddered on the ground, limbs thumping.

"Fool dwarf. Not ridden, not cursed. Wedded, blessed are we."

Tomza snapped the duabuw to her shoulder when she saw a trio of shades prowling through the fog. Unlike the previous three, these came boldly toward her. Bright eyes flashed a venomous yellow in darkly furred faces. Thin lips parted around too-wide mouths stuffed with an excess of teeth. It was a predator's smile, but it held malice that no natural beast could have mustered.

The wrongness of the creatures stoked a hidden but deep spike of hatred in the dwarf, and she rallied her flagging courage around its hot strength. She could hear the first two attackers moving somewhere behind her in the mist. She and Waelon were done for, but she was not about to go down without a bloody fight.

"I didn't think even a wheezer would sink so low," she snarled. "But I suppose the wight sent you to die, so maybe it understands what you are."

Laughs spilled from the three gremalkins like guts from a sliced belly. They spread out, daring Tomza to direct her attention to one of them and expose her flank.

"Dreamers remember," the centermost creature said. "And as cold dreamers remember, so bloody Mother remembers old things and wild things."

Tomza heard a scuff on the stone beside her, but before she could turn around, a broad hand gripped her shoulder for support. She felt the pain in every syllable as Waelon spoke, yet his words were all the stronger for it.

"Feelin' curious, pussycat?" he taunted. "Stop your chatterin' and let's finish this dance. I've got a brother waitin'."

In answer, the lead beast sniffed the air, then gave a low, wet growl. The gremalkins' smiles got wider, and the eyes of all five creatures bored into Tomza.

"Dwarf knows it," the leader whispered seductively. "Has felt the waking. Known the touch. Bears it in the blood."

"*NO!*"

The cry tore from Tomza's throat with a force she could not understand, and her finger clenched around the trigger.

The shot was not a good one since her body was wracked by fear and wrath, but her shout surprised the leading gremalkin. It started, and its outthrust head jerked backward in shock. Ill-favor for the goblin skin-changer or providence on behalf of the dwarfess; it wasn't clear. A bolt lodged in the gremalkin's skull, and it twisted in its death throes.

Tomza adjusted her grip to wield her crossbow as a club again, but her attackers came on too quickly. A leaping kick knocked the weapon from her grip, and a lunge dragged claws through her sturdy boots to pull her legs out from under her. She screamed and reached for her sword, kicking at the creature pulling her legs. She sensed one coming in for the kill, but Waelon's axe swing caught it between its shoulders. Its clawed limb dangled as blood splashed across her face. Waelon tumbled sideways with a pained scream when another crashed into him.

Tomza's hand settled on her magsax, but the creature at her legs found a chink in her armor. She cried out, her hand pinned by a claw as a huge maw yawned toward her face.

She wanted to look away from the bite that would rip her face off her skull, but stubbornness demanded she meet her end glaring defiance.

The gremalkin's mouth stopped inches short of her nose, and

the creature's choked gasp was so gross that it made Tomza's eyes water and her gorge rise. Then she saw its tongue retract through the back of its skull, pulled out by a leaf-bladed sword clutched in long, dark hands.

"Hold still, sweet maiden," Utyrvaul warned as the sword licked out at the gremalkin pinning her legs. "There we are. Now, if you would be so kind as to get up?"

Tomza lay blinking, then the *thwack* of a duabuw reached her ears. She saw Commander Torbjorn trudging toward her while working the lever of his crossbow with mechanical precision.

"On your feet, Ascedwan," the dwarf declared, then loosed another shot. It was rewarded by a keening cry. "I need you to help Waelon."

A dark shape rushed in from her side, but the svartalf's blade whistled through the air. The creature lurched back, screeching in pain and thwarted rage.

"Now, Tomza."

Her body hurt in ways and places her mind hadn't yet come to grips with, but the dwarfess rallied to the stern voice and got to her feet. Casting about, she saw Waelon, his face like chalk as he fought for every breath. Her limbs were leaden and her whole body burned, but she shambled over quickly and forced herself to crouch under the ranger's arm.

Waelon's agonized gasps repeated a single word.

"Raelon... Raelon... Raelon..."

The chanted name drove ice into her veins.

"Tell that brother of yours that he's going to have to wait a bit longer," Tomza said.

Waelon moaned with each step, halting his recitation. Behind them, the efforts of the dwarf and svartalf rearguard sent cries of pain and death ringing across the stony cliffs.

"That's right," Tomza panted in the stricken ranger's ear. "You tell Raelon I'm not hauling your arse across this mountain for nothing. He's going to be waiting a good long time."

CHAPTER THREE

"I've got him, lass. You can let go."

Tomza stared at Haeda. The words made sense separately, but together, they muddled up.

Let go? Let go of what? She wasn't holding any—

The veil of fatigue rose enough for her to realize her body felt heavy because she was still half-carrying, half-dragging Waelon. She looked from Waelon's slack, pale face to his heavy arm draped limply across her shoulder, and her heart seized in her chest. Had it all been for nothing? How long had she been carrying a dead body?

She didn't let go of him so much as collapse away from him. She surrendered herself to the fall, and the ground rushed up to meet her. Then strong hands caught her and gently lowered her the rest of the way. A sky the color of slate spread over her, and then she saw a familiar silhouette breaching the vast deep gray infinity.

"It's okay," Ober told her. "You made it. You're safe."

Tomza shook her head, her mind tangled up. How she could be safe when the memories were all still with her, chasing each other around her skull?

"I tried," she began.

From beside her came a guttural groan. Impossibly, it sounded like Waelon, but the ranger was dead, wasn't he?

"Waelon," Tomza tried again, "I tried to...to save him..."

Her throat tightened and her voice faded.

"Ribs are broken." Haeda sniffed. "Fool's lucky he didn't drive a spur into his lungs."

"What are we going to do?" Gromic rumbled, his tone so low that Tomza felt it in her chest. "He's in no shape to move."

"Waelon's dead." Tomza sobbed. "I tried."

"No, no, he's going to be okay." Ober's hands settled on either side of her face. "He's hurt, but he's going to be okay. You did good, Dwan."

Tomza was confused. Hadn't she seen his bloodless, unmoving face? Fear, weariness, and pain had worn her as smooth as a river stone, but she'd seen it, hadn't she?

Tomza sat up enough to break free of Ober's hands, looking to where Haeda's and Gromic's voices had come from. Barely two strides away, the older dwarfess and her large companion bent over Waelon's body. Her brother shushed her and tried to get her to lie back down, but she ignored him. She watched Waelon's barrel chest rise and fall, catching every so often with a pained hitch.

"Tomza!" Ober exclaimed, his voice sharp with alarm. "You're hurt."

She looked at her brother, who was holding up a blood-smeared hand as a testament to her injury. She had a fleeting memory of the raking claw, but in the face of the incredible relief at Waelon's survival, the injury was comical.

"Pussycat gave me a scratch." She giggled. "Gave a few of them more than a scratch though, hehe."

Ober stared at her with a mixture of shock and relief. If she was laughing while holding herself up, she couldn't be hurt that badly.

"You stay here," he said, patting the ground with a bloody hand. "I'm going to get some water to clean that scratch of yours."

The idea of leaving her spot on the ground was more hilarious than her injury, and the young dwarfess gave a resounding croak of laughter. "Take your time I'm…ha-ha…not going anywhere!"

Ober's expression was somewhere between a forced smile and a worried frown as he shuffled off.

Still chuckling, she sank back. She was keenly aware of every flaming fiber of muscle in her neck, shoulders, and back. She'd run a race the likes of which she could not have imagined, and she'd not only survived but she'd won. When she relaxed, every ache and pain made itself known. She was tired and strained almost beyond endurance, and that enhanced the victory.

She told herself that if a clacker strode forward to plant a spear in her, she would die smiling. She'd won, and they couldn't take that from her.

It seemed like the Wyrd was going to test her hypothesis when a tall figure loomed over her. Her breath caught, and every tortured muscle seized.

But the eyes of the tall figure possessed no unhallowed light, only a reddish gleam above a grinning mouth full of sharp, bright teeth.

"So good to see you made it, my dear," Utyrvaul said. "For a time, I was concerned that even the fabled dwarf constitution would not be able to carry on, considering your previous efforts and the burden you bore. I'm pleased that I was wrong."

A gruff voice heralded a far shorter, wider figure.

"A true dwarvish woman is made of stone and iron, eh, Dwan?" Torbjorn said. "I wouldn't expect anything less from any of my dwan, even if they had the misfortune of being one of those clay-toed Valeborn."

Tomza matched the twinkle in her commander's eye with a smile and a wink, then managed a stiff salute.

"Glad to barely meet expectations as always, Commander."

Torbjorn gave an amused snort and glanced at the face of the foggy mountain they'd just crossed.

"Any movement worth noting?" he asked, half-turning to the svartalf beside him.

The elf's keen eyes roved in the indicated direction. When he completed his inspection, a smile tugged at the corners of Utyrvaul's mouth.

"Nothing we need worry about," he declared, cocking his head to one side and listening. "Though I can still hear the bellicose dead urging the bulk of their forces toward this arm of the mountain. It seems they did not appreciate the summary devastation of their patrol."

"I wouldn't expect anything less." Torbjorn sighed. "How long do we have?"

The svartalf was looking down the slope they were on. Torbjorn repeated the question to get his attention.

"Hm, well, I'd say we have a few hours," he replied. "Perhaps a little longer with the light failing. Their human auxiliaries are just beginning to bumble about, but the mist, wind, and stone are giving them fits. Once they lose the light, they'll be lucky not to lose their footing and slide back down on their masters below."

"Good riddance," Ober said, returning to clean Tomza's wounds. "Hope the wheezer mounts their heads on pikes for what they did to my sister."

Tomza tried to rouse enough to correct her brother, but Utyrvaul, as quick as ever, spared her the effort.

"Oh, it wasn't the poor midges who waylaid your dear sister. The nefarious assault was perpetrated by none other than the *Sith'Ceilicairn*. Nasty creatures."

Ober had gingerly turned Tomza's head to one side and was dabbing gently with the wet rag. Tomza found the cool touch of the moist fabric to be a welcome balm.

"Gremalkin." Torbjorn grunted, arms crossed over his broad chest. "Goblin skin-changers."

Ober started at the mention of the spirit-ridden, and Tomza took a sharp breath when he pressed the cloth hard against her open wound.

"Sorry." Ober hastily resumed his gentle dabbing and raised his gaze to his commander. "Goblin skin-changers? I've never heard of anything like that."

"Far from common," Utyrvaul remarked. "The bestial spirits prefer longer-lived creatures for occupation, but the more bloodthirsty ones find the opportunity to hunt and kill worth the effort, I suppose."

"Mine feels bloodthirsty enough," Ober muttered under his breath, shame and defiance hardening his face. Tomza saw his expression from the corner of her eye, and her good humor withered on the vine.

Her brother's affliction had saved them not long ago, but her encounter with the gremalkins was an uncomfortable reminder. The curse he bore was so unnatural that even the sight of other skin-changers had provoked a deep loathing in Tomza at their wrongness. She could tell herself it was because they were goblins or that they rejoiced in their affliction and being used as hunting beasts for unliving masters, but to be spirit-ridden was to be anathema, and as far anyone knew, irrevocably so.

With those thoughts running through her weary mind, the glow of surviving grew cold. Bone-deep exhaustion settled over her.

"I only encountered them once before when we were clearing the southern Vale before the wheezers," Torbjorn continued. "We'd been commanded to pacify a grem warren in the marshes south of Waelleton. En route, our baggage train was hit by a pack of the creatures. We wheeled into formation, mud sucking at our boots, but they were gone.

"After waiting for near on two hours, we set off again, and

they hit another part of the line. Ended up losing over two score of dwan before we adjusted our marching order to keep the sneaks at bay with salvos of bolts. Put down nearly a dozen the next time they had a go, and after that, it seemed that whatever help they owed the warren was considered paid in full."

"Damn!" Ober exclaimed. "What happened when you got to the warren?"

Torbjorn's gaze sharpened, and the young dwarf looked away.

"What happened?" the dwarf commander growled, then caught himself and sagged into a deep sigh. "What always happened when a bunch of armed dwarfs marched into a goblin warren?"

Ober, eyes still downcast, nodded and fought to clear his throat.

"Yes, sir." He coughed. "Sorry, sir."

Torbjorn looked as though he wanted to say something, but the attention of all present was drawn to a sudden pained yelp. Waelon had been stripped to his smallclothes, and Gromic held him in a sitting position. Just behind him, Haeda hauled on leather straps connected to a band of canvas that was wrapped around Waelon's burly frame. The pungent, earthy smell of one of Tomza's poultices filled the air as liquid seeped between the tightening folds.

"You shameless, heartless witch," Waelon snarled breathlessly at Haeda. "What are you doing to m...*agh*!"

Throwing her not inconsiderable weight into the effort, Haeda drew the leather straps even tighter, and more poultice gunk slid free.

"You just be glad I've got muscles and a fine set of hips." Haeda set about securing the leather straps. "Otherwise, you'd have nothing to hold your old bird bones together but whatever scraps of cloth we could scrounge from Gromic's tattered smallclothes."

"Trust me, Waelon," the stout dwarf chuckled. "The poultice stink would've been the least of your worries."

Utyrvaul's smile was shark-like as he danced forward to look the corset-swaddled dwarf over.

"Oh, Master Davish, you look stunning!" He basked in the big dwarf's glare. "Why, you will be the envy of all the ladies at the ball, I assure you."

The other dwarfs couldn't keep their snickers from escaping.

"You're dead, elf," Waelon hissed after an abortive attempt to sit up. "You just don't know it yet."

"Oh, we're all dying, my lovely." The svartalf giggled. "But promise me that you and I will get at least one dance in this stunning outfit before it's over."

The choked laughs from the Bad Badgers turned into howls when Utyrvaul sprang back after the ranger's meaty hand nearly seized his thin neck.

"Enough flirting, you two. We've got to get things sorted," Torbjorn chided. "Wait, where's the girl?"

The good humor of the group bled out fast in the gathering dark. Their eyes swept over the mountain path, the discarded weapons, and the packs that had been abandoned as the wounded rounded the bend. The child with the golden eyes, the crux upon which their mad mission behind enemy lines was based, was nowhere to be seen.

"I left her sitting next to my pack," Haeda began, panic sharpening each word. "She was barely awake, so I thought—"

"To hell with what you thought," Torbjorn barked, scanning the growing darkness. "Find her *now*!"

CHAPTER FOUR

There were times when she felt...old.

She knew it was a silly thought, given that she was a little girl, but it tickled the back of her mind. She told herself she needed to pick it out of her mind and throw it away, but she couldn't. Thoughts were like the old webs of the holy spinners in her grandmother's palace, sticky and stubborn.

Her memories were part of that sticky web—strand after strand connected by the thinnest filaments to places and people she couldn't name. For instance, she could remember Grandmother's palace, spider-haunted and shadow-bound, but even when she squeezed her eyes shut to the point of tears, she couldn't recall much. She knew the palace had a name and she'd spent time there with Grandmother, but so much was lost.

It was painful and maddening, but worse was what she'd come to call the holes in the world. She'd seen the first one when she emerged from under the mountain with the funny people and looked at the Stone Key. She didn't know why or how she knew it was called that, and what she didn't see when she looked around was distressing.

There were patterned lines dug into the ground, but there had once been a vast complex of walls and corridors where…well, where something happened. The shock of feeling that she knew the place and seeing it not just broken or falling down but gone was quieter and more awful.

She thought about what she'd seen and stewed in the sense of dread and wrongness. Things should not be this way, and the longer she traveled with the funny people, the more they encountered such places. Especially here among the mountains, where she could see that the high towers no longer grew from the forested floor and the sprawling palaces no longer overhung the blunt peaks. Over and over, she saw vacancies, and they made her want to hide. To run back to the place beneath the mountain and crawl back inside the terrible glass box. It had been cold and stiff in there and impossible to stay awake for very long. The box now seemed a place of cold comfort compared to the vandalized world she faced every new day of traveling.

Her reverie was broken as she thought about her new traveling companions, then heard the stomping of their boots coming down the mountain path toward her. To entertain herself during the tedious parts of their trip, she'd memorized the sounds of their feet on the stone, along with the smell of each, earthy and rich, with subtle differences. That had occupied her for hours as they huddled around the campfire.

When she tilted her head to one side, listening, then sniffed the breeze, she'd known who was coming to find her, and she smiled.

In the lead was the one called Haeda, who she knew to be female. Everything womanly about her was squashed down and dense, however. Despite that, she thought Haeda was very pretty, though not in the way Mother and maybe Grandmother had been. The funny woman was gentle and spoke softly and was quick to wrap her in a warm embrace when she felt afraid or cold.

Behind her came Gromic, his puffing breath as telltale as the heavy stomp of his feet. She liked him too. When she was tired or just because the mood took him, he would scoop her up and carry her. Sometimes it was in his arms, her body curling against his huge chest. Other times, she would be swung up to sit astride his shoulders, where she could drum her finger atop his helmet. The songs she tapped had words she couldn't remember, and sometimes that made her sad, but most often, it felt good to hear the familiar rhythms. He also pulled faces while cooking, and those made her giggle. His bushy face looked ridiculous when lit by the flames.

The two would find her soon standing here, looking down the slope toward the valley. She'd been here long enough that she'd forgotten what was so striking as to hold her in this position.

She squinted into the darkness. The track wound down and down the mountain, sometimes curling in on itself to switch back and twisting lower still. Nothing had been familiar about this lonely stretch, but then the wind had stirred the fog, and it had shifted enough that she could just make out faint glows on the valley floor. She stood staring at the shrouded lights.

Yes, those were what had drawn her from beside Haeda's pack. Eyes roaming and mind wandering, she'd caught the lights as night fell, and they had stirred another incomplete memory. The mist shifted with the dropping temperature, settling lower, and the lights in the valley had vanished. She decided then and there that she wasn't done looking at them.

The dwarfs were busy about their own affairs, so she'd slipped off to see if she could get a better view. She thought they might be the lights of a town, but she struggled to imagine any bastion of civilization that made do with such meager light. Also, the light seemed...wrong. It was more like the glow that came from a campfire. The people down there couldn't be keeping everything lit by burning things indoors, could they? That sounded smoky and smelly and, well, dangerous. Like something primitives would do.

Reflecting upon the lights below and remembering the word "primitives" had pinned her to this spot. The flavor of the word at the back of her mind was not good, but she couldn't remember why. The overtones were "dirty" or "embarrassing," but it didn't have the punch or tingle of anything really bad.

She knew it was unusual that she hadn't spoken since the funny people had found her. She wondered why she hadn't. She had not understood the strange tongue of the funny people at first. She could've spoken to see if they understood her, but the thought of it made the words buzz at the back of her throat and her mind twist in on itself.

She knew that if she spoke, something would happen. She knew it would be bad without knowing why, so she'd kept quiet, her many thoughts her own. She had been keen to listen to them, though, and learn their language.

It had been strangely familiar, reminding her of things that hummed in the dark corners of Grandmother's palace. As she'd explored further, she'd found there were twists and turns of phrase beyond her understanding. Still, she was good at languages, or she remembered being so, and she had nothing better to do. Clinging to every word, she now had a working vocabulary.

When Haeda's voice rose in a cry of relief, the ensuing sounds made sense to her. She was aware it was an imperfect translation, however.

"Thank Rocks," the female called as she waddled over, as the squat beings were prone to do. "I felt fear much. Why thing do, Gehrl?"

She blinked, shaken from her thoughts, and Haeda's strong hands dragged her into an embrace.

"Why thing do, Gehrl? Much, much fear me, Gehrl."

She smiled at their name for her. It was guttural and blunt but somehow seemed fitting. She didn't mind it. It served when she didn't know her own name. That should have concerned her more, but recently, she'd been thinking of herself as "Gehrl."

"Rocks be good!" Gromic puffed as he came up behind Haeda and settled a heavy but affectionate hand atop her head. "I and more fear much felt. Seeing makes happy me."

She grinned at his round flushed cheeks and felt a giggle rising, though she knew they weren't amused. Haeda's hands tightened. The female's grip was not painful, but the sense of demanding urgency was not lost on her.

"Why thing do, Gehrl? Why?"

Her predicament involving speech was most difficult in these moments when the funny people pressed her to explain something. A smile or gesture would satisfy them most of the time. At other times, though, she employed a pantomime to communicate enough to forestall their questioning.

This was not one of those times. The problem was two-fold, the first being her handicap. Second, even if she could speak without the bad thing happening, she would have been hard-pressed to put into words why she had been staring down into the valley.

She was, after all, just a little girl, though a very clever one.

So, she bore their stares for as long as she could, then made the paltry offering of pointing at the valley floor where the strange glows could be seen. They followed the line of her finger, and they both drew a sharp breath. The pair exchanged words so quickly and quietly that she had a hard time following the rushing slur of words. She did hear names, Torbjorn and Waelon, in the conversation. The name Utyrvaul came up, and she felt a shudder pass through her that had nothing to do with the cold.

That creature was not a funny person but a scary one. He made her want to go back into the glass box, especially when he looked at her with those glittering red eyes.

She instinctively pressed closer to Haeda, and with a movement that felt just as instinctive, the female accepted her, welcoming her weight.

"Good Gehrl," Haeda breathed as she turned from Gromic. "No scare this. Safe you. Good Gehrl."

Safe you.

Hidden within the folds of Haeda's cloak and held tightly, with her eyes squeezed tight and her face pressed to Haeda's warm, earthy smell, she almost believed it.

CHAPTER FIVE

"I didn't think I'd ever be so happy to see a human."

Torbjorn gave a grunt of acknowledgment at Waelon's wheezed statement as they watched Gromic tote the girl back up the path. Haeda trotted so close behind that she looked like she might hop on Gromic's back.

"Strange times," the commander said.

The big dwarf was getting what little rest he could in his current state. Every breath was a pained wheeze, and he perpetually scowled down at the corset. Torbjorn saw that Waelon was getting some color back in his face. He tried not to think about their need to be on the move again and the question of the ranger's fitness to travel.

Shall we cast ourselves on witchery again?

"We really ought to come up with a name for her," Torbjorn muttered. "I'd hoped by now she'd tell us what to call her, but I'm beginning to wonder if she'll ever speak. We might as well come up with a name."

"Why bother?" Waelon croaked with a pained laugh. "Afraid someone's going to get confused about who you're talking to?"

Torbjorn shrugged. It was a fair point. The other person

among the Bad Badgers who might also be classified as a "girl" was Tomza, and it would be beneath Torbjorn and her dignity to call her that. She was a dwan, as worthy of the name as any he'd served with, despite her…peculiar behaviors.

"Tomza and Ober back yet?" Waelon asked, attempting to raise himself using the boulder to look around.

"No." The commander sighed. "Though I don't imagine they've ranged far. Hauling your carcass nearly did that lass in, I think."

The ranger gave a snort that prompted another wince. "Wasn't the only thing. Girl had to fight off a clacker too. That would have been enough, but then the lass had to face those gremalkins. Say what you want about her, but there's iron in that dwan."

Torbjorn turned to the surly ranger in surprise. "Are we in the last days before the hammer stroke sunders the failed earth?" he demanded. "That was the first time you've ever complimented a fellow dwan."

Waelon adjusted his position against the boulder and choked back a soft cry of pain.

"Must have busted more than my ribs," the big dwarf muttered under his breath. "Don't go telling a soul, or they'll think I've gone soft."

"Not a chance," Torbjorn promised as he stepped forward to receive the successful trackers. "Where did you find her?"

"Not far from here." Gromic came to a stop and lowered his burden to the ground. "Seems she spotted something worth investigating and wanted to get a better look."

Torbjorn frowned at the golden-eyed human child, mustache twitching.

"She told you that?"

"Well, uh, not exactly, sir," Gromic explained. "You see, sir, we found her standin' a little ways on, and when Haeda asked the little rascal why she'd run off, the girl pointed."

"Pointed?" the leader of the Bad Badgers asked, and when the stout blond dwarf stalled in his explanation, Torbjorn's gaze swung to the female. "Haeda?"

"I think she spotted the lights of a town down the slope," she explained. "They must have just been lighting up to drive out the night when she spied them through the fog. Better eyes than an elf sniper, this one."

Haeda's hand fell affectionately on the girl's shoulder, and the child tucked herself behind Gromic's formidable frame.

"Oh, I'm not sure we need to exaggerate that much," came a soft-voiced drawl from behind Torbjorn. "The child could be a prodigy by human or even dwarvish standards without sullying the reputation of elvish sharpshooters."

Utyrvaul strolled into camp.

"And you're so keen-eyed that you saw through stone to know to come back without doing a proper sweep for the girl?" Waelon remarked dryly.

"No, of course not, silly." The elf giggled, savoring the ranger's grimace at the sound. "But it isn't just our eyes that are keen. These blade-ears are good for something, eh, Commander?"

Torbjorn wasn't embarrassed.

"You made it back just in time," he remarked, noting how the girl watched the elf with an unwavering and terrified gaze. "You can prance back out into the dark and fetch our young compatriots. Can't imagine they've gotten far, given the state young Tomza was in."

"And yet you sent her into the night with enemies all about." Utyrvaul tutted, then turned on his heel to head into the mist-wreathed dark. "Don't run off without us. My delicate frame is not made for portaging dwarfs."

Waelon barely waited for half a heartbeat before he hawked and spat after the svartalf.

"His bony arse ain't fit for much besides a good kickin' if you ask me."

No one said anything but a high, sing-song voice called back from somewhere in the mists. "Yet, no one did ask, did they, Master Waelon?"

Gromic stifled a low chuckle but gave up trying to hide his mirth when he saw Waelon's withering glare. Haeda, too busy adjusting the lass' patchwork cloak, gave them little attention. Torbjorn was likewise fixated on the child, but it was not her hair or warmth that concerned him. She had a haunted look in her large golden eyes as she stared at where the elf had vanished.

Svartalfs were striking creatures, from their height to their red eyes and needle teeth in their midnight-shaded faces. Torbjorn remembered when he'd first seen one of their princes arrive at the royal domicile many long years ago. He had been nearly an infant by the reckoning of his people, a tender three or four years old, so no one had raised issue when he'd hidden behind his mother's skirt. It was like seeing one of the nightmare princes of the Arcadi Wylds from cribside tales come to life. Even now, when those red eyes met his, Torbjorn wondered what sort of machinations were woven in those foreign minds. Nothing good was what he always surmised.

Yet for all that, the girl had traveled with Utyrvaul for days. She'd occasionally eaten game he'd brought down along the way and been watched by him on nights when the svartalf stood guard with one of the dwarfs. None of this dulled her unease.

The dwarf commander wondered what lay behind the girl's strange eyes as well. For all their youth, those eyes had opened inside a chamber as old as the foundations of his people's empire. There was something just as unsettling behind that youthful face as any elf's.

You already cast that die and can't take back the roll.

Torbjorn cleared his throat sharply to signal he was done musing and the rest needed to listen.

"You say she spotted a town, but did you see it too?" he

inquired as his hand wandered to his pocket where Klaus' map sat. "And if you spied it, how far is it from our current position?"

"Aye, we saw it, sir," Gromic eagerly confirmed. His brow knotted as he began the laborious process of calculating the distance before casting a surreptitious look at Haeda. The dwarfess gave a disgusted sigh and rolled her eyes.

"A day's march down the track will see us reaching its outskirts," she stated confidently. "That's without the walking wounded, mind you. With everyone hale, we could cut that time in half, and I could have my team there in a few hours."

The last was a wistful reminder that Haeda, despite her preoccupation with the human child, hadn't forgotten her beloved worcsvine. Torbjorn wanted to take the time to commiserate on the loss of her faithful beasts, which had probably fed the wight's auxiliary forces, but they had enemies breathing down their necks and an unknown quantity in their path to escape said enemy. Grinding his teeth, he unfolded the map and traced their planned path off Turoth's Tooth. Assuming he wasn't off much in his estimation of their position, there was only one option for which community the girl had spied.

"Well, looks like that's Paelon's Watch," Torbjorn's subterranean-attuned eyes deciphered the map in the sickly moonlight. "That or we're really confused, and you spotted the town of Cremplewash down there. Didn't happen to see a river running by it, did you?"

"Fog was thick," Gromic began, but a shake of Haeda's head made up his mind for him. "But no river."

"Small mercies," the dwarf commander murmured, folding the map to put it back in his pocket.

"Paelon's Watch is older than the settling, but it's got dwarvish roots," Haeda offered. "Might be some of those old, deep places we could find some friendly stone to hunker down in."

"Maybe," Torbjorn agreed. "But it's been under wheezer control for a good long while, which means there's a good chance that the folk there will raise the alarm at the sight of us. Not looking to find trouble ahead when I've got trouble behind."

They lapsed into silence as the leader of the Bad Badgers mulled their options. More than once, he caught Gromic's and Haeda's eyes drifting to Waelon, but neither would do the dwan the dishonor of pointing out his compromised state in front of him. They didn't have to; Torbjorn knew what the reality was. The choice might soon be before him, and he glanced at Waelon. The ranger knew and had accepted it.

They stood around in the dark, none daring to settle in, certain that things would turn soon. They knew catching a few minutes of sleep would be impossible even for seasoned veterans like them.

Their wait ended when they heard a soft whistle. The girl shrank against Gromic.

"Come along, dearies. Back to the comforts of kith and kin we go," Utyrvaul said with a rapacious grin. "Oh, these poor darlings were all sorts of turned around, and if I hadn't found them, they would have wandered right off a cliff."

Ober, supporting a limping Tomza, emerged from the fog, their faces dark with their blushes. "Sorry, sir. Got turned around in the fog, and I led her—"

"Oh, shut up, Ober," she snarled. "You know I managed to twist the kak out of my ankle all on my own, so don't be taking any of the credit."

Haeda looked meaningfully at Torbjorn, who returned the look with a heavy sigh and a shake of his head.

"Tomza..." He coughed, forcing the words around a tightening in his throat. "You wouldn't be able to work any of your... well, that business you do... That is, can you do that for yourself and Waelon?"

The big dwarf protested, but Torbjorn silenced him with a wave and kept watching Tomza. He wanted her to do what was right and proper and tell him she would never do such a thing again and she was sorry she ever disgraced herself so, but a deeper, harder part of him desperately wanted to see her answer by drawing out her flint knife and bowl.

"Commander, I..." Tomza's voice trailed off as she looked at Waelon and then down at her swelling ankle. "I can try, but—"

"It might kill her," Ober finished. "That, or it could make things worse for both of them."

Torbjorn looked at Tomza, hoping against hope that she was about to correct her brother by cursing him for a fool who didn't know the difference between blood magic and button mushrooms. Yet, she only met Torbjorn's eyes, her gaze promising she would try if he asked it of her, even though she had faced a lifetime of fear, pain, and death today.

Torbjorn's thumb slid over his scarred cheek, and he swallowed hard.

Into the belly of the beast, then.

"All right," he declared, straightening as his tone took on the timbre of command. "Do what needs doing and gather what needs gathering, then we'll go look for some friendly stone."

His eye wandered to the human girl, who gave a large yawn as she returned his gaze, golden eyes reflecting the watery moonlight.

"And no wandering off," he finished with a wink.

CHAPTER SIX

"We've got a problem."

Torbjorn clamped his jaw shut to keep from snarling a rebuke at the redundant observation. Instead, he busied himself with scanning the path they were on, assessing their options for cover. The dwarfs beside him drooped with fatigue. The tentative hues of rosy dawn were filtering through the sky. They trudged down the rough mountain track all night, sometimes carrying the wounded.

They were in no condition to run or fight, yet coming up the path was a troop of humans. They looked to be a militia, bearing eclectic arms and in a ragged formation. They seemed not to have spotted the dwarfs yet, but it was only a matter of minutes until the longshanks would be upon the beleaguered Bad Badgers.

"Think they're here for us?" Ober asked. He was at his sister's side. "To hold us up while the wheezer's forces come from behind."

Torbjorn was too busy assessing his paltry options to reply.

"More like their magistrate heard the ruckus and sent them to investigate," Gromic said, adjusting his grip on Waelon. "A bunch of slack-jaws. Hardly the types you'd send if you thought it was worth the time of anyone serious."

Slack-jawed or not, the approaching militia outnumbered them two to one and despite their groggy disposition, Torbjorn doubted they'd spent the past twelve hours running for their lives while carrying wounded comrades. This was a fight they neither needed nor wanted, but the possibility of avoiding it was slim.

The dwarf commander's eyes shifted to Utyrvaul. The svartalf was looking at him expectantly. There was a desperate gambit to be played here, and while it was unlikely to work, given their few options, it seemed the only possibility that wouldn't immediately end in violence.

Still, having the svartalf thinking the same thing did little to ease Torbjorn's mind.

"I'm trusting you not to press your advantage, elf," he rumbled, ignoring the concerned looks from his dwarfs. "We're in a tight spot, but not so tight that my finger can't pull a trigger."

Utyrvaul adopted an exaggerated expression of sorrow.

"Torbjorn, really! After all we have been through together!" he whined, his thin lips trembling piteously. "That you would even suggest a thing wounds me. It really does."

"You'll get over it," Torbjorn growled, then leaned close so only the myrkling could hear. "Remember, should things get desperate, Ober is likely to change. Then we are all as good as dead."

For the first time, the sober expression flashing across the svartalf's face was genuine.

"That...that is a fair point."

Mabon Reeve wasn't happy about being sent on this errand by the magistrate, and he most certainly wasn't happy about who he'd been sent with.

"We should've taken the northern fork," Ferren muttered to the man next to him, just loud enough that the patrol leader could hear. "Would've been an easier climb and gives time for the sun to clear up the fog."

Mabon considered turning around and giving the man a piece of his mind but settled for choking back a growl and swiping a thin line of perspiration from his brow. It didn't matter that the southern fork gave them a more direct path over the arm or that it didn't have them running under several cliffs that would make a perfect spot for an ambush.

It didn't even matter that the magistrate had been very clear that this was to be done quickly so Paelon's Watch could be ready to receive a wight lord if one was heading their way. No, not a bit of it would matter to Ferren Bowen since the forester was hungover and prone to insubordination at the best of times. Combine that with the reality that most of the men with them saw Mabon as a child elevated above his station, and he understood how this would play out.

Mabon hoped to keep it together long enough to find the wight lord's vanguard if that was indeed who was raising a racket along the mountain's arm. He imagined that Ferren and his cronies wouldn't grumble so loud when faced with real soldiers. They might not embarrass him, but Mabon wasn't going to hold his breath.

Glancing up the slope to check their progress, the young man nearly cried out in shock when a tall, dark figure emerged from the mist, leading a string of squat, hunched figures in drab gray cloaks.

"Hold up," Mabon called behind him, and the unwieldy patrol staggered to a halt, weapons not being drawn so much as drifting into clumsy hands.

"Nearly bumped into 'em, didn't we?" Ferren groused as he strung his bow with a grunt. "If I'd been in the front, don't imagine that would have happened."

Mabon's face burned. It was sloppy of him, but none of the rest of them had been any better, and the fog was still thick. Swallowing his doubts, he took the sword on his belt firmly in hand. The first rays of dawn caught the edge, turning the blade into a flashing tongue of flame. Mabon called out in his best impression of a commanding voice.

"Halt! Who goes there?" he cried, and for an instant, Ferren couldn't hide his surprise.

The lad had a strong pair of lungs.

The tall figure stepped forward, hands upraised. The gray shapes behind him shuffled dutifully in his wake.

"At ease, good Captain," came the silken voice of a highbrow svartalf. "We mean you no harm. I am but a humble merchant with my—"

"I said, *halt!*" Mabon bellowed, eyeing the bowmen in the patrol with a nod to signal them to be prepared to loose. "Hold still, or you'll be sporting new feathers."

The elf froze, hands still upraised. His face split into a brittle, apologetic smile.

"Terribly sorry. We've just been through a trial," the svartalf declared with a voice so tremulous it bordered on a sob, his smile holding on by a thread. "First there was the rockslide that injured two of my servants, and then we had to get out of the way of the army after an officer dismissed us. My nerves are just shot, and I'm not quite myself."

Mabon's eyes narrowed. Two of the stooped figures were indeed being helped to stand by their fellows. Each was nearly bent double with a heavy load. The poor wretches pondered the ground from beneath drooping hoods. Mabon was as impatient as any young man, but he was not of a cruel disposition. He looked behind him and thought about how he would hate to have to limp the rest of the way to the city if he were injured.

"You said you encountered an officer of the army?" he asked. "Is a wight lord's army on the march?"

The svartalf affected a shrug that made his shoulders sink.

"I'm sorry, but I don't rightly know since my instructions came from a goblin officer who seemed to be head of the vanguard. He was keen to have us out of the way of the main force and made it clear that our safety was not promised if we lingered in their path. I'm a traveling merchant by trade, not a soldier like you rugged warriors."

Mabon's patrol gave a soft chuff of pleasure at the flattery, but the young man felt certain there was a barb tucked into the compliment. He might be young, but by his father's sword, he wouldn't be reeled in like a fish.

"I see you have important business," the svartalf continued. "We shall move out of your way so you can—"

"I haven't given you permission to move, elf," Mabon snapped, the sharpness of his tone pinning the tall figure where he stood. "What business do you have roaming these mountains?"

From behind him, Mabon heard a mutter.

"Didn't you hear him, you daft bastard? He says he's a merchant." Ferren scoffed, and Mabon noted the affirmative grunts among his men.

The elf shot a quick glance at the young man and the archer loitering at the back of the patrol, but when he spoke, his voice was placating.

"My apologies once more, good Captain. Again, I forget myself out of fatigue," he continued, his head bobbing in deference. "As I've said, I am a merchant, and I've come looking for communities in need of my services."

As Mabon gathered himself to speak, the men began to seethe. They had swallowed the elf's story. He was as anxious as any of them to see their duty discharged—he had business of his own to attend to—but the magistrate had chosen him for this task, and he wouldn't do a sloppy job just because some drunks moaned at him.

"What are those services?" he pressed.

"Oh, come off it, Mabon," Ferren called loudly enough that every eye turned toward him. He was leaning on his bow, arrow dangling from his fist. "They're clearly not a threat, and we've still got half a mountain to climb. Let the poor bastards go on their way so we can get this over with."

Mabon bit back the reply that surged into his mouth when he saw the mutinous gleam in more than a few eyes. He breathed through his nostrils, hating how it whistled. When he spoke, there was more control in his tone than he felt.

"The magistrate chose me to lead this patrol," he enunciated clearly. "If you disagree with his choice, feel free to let him know when we return to town."

The thought of facing the magistrate of Paelon's Watch was enough to drain the color out of the faces of most of the men facing Mabon.

Not Ferren Bowen. He showed his contempt by affecting an exaggerated yawn.

"I'm terribly sorry to be the cause of such consternation," the svartalf called. "If it makes any better, I will swear to go directly to your magistrate when we reach your fine town. We'll just have to shuffle past you to get there…"

"Don't you move a muscle, myrkling," Mabon shouted, continuing to pin Ferren with his eyes. "We'll escort you to town, where we will hand you over to the Guard before returning to our duties."

Ferren hawked and spat at the announcement, and Mabon heard more than a few mumbles of discontent. Mabon met each man's eyes, but none dared raise a complaint.

"Master Bowen," Mabon called, a hard, humorless smile on his face. "Will you please secure the prisoners?"

For an instant, Mabon could see the battle being waged within the archer's mind—his contempt for Mabon fighting his fear of the repercussions. Mabon would never know the results of that battle since the man's head snapped back and he fell to the ground, his stiffening legs doing a final jig. Mabon's eyes registered the bolt jutting from the dead man's skull before his mind could comprehend its significance, and in that time, three more of his men crumpled. One sported a similar skull ornament, and the other pair was pierced by one arrow.

Mabon swung around with a cry that was part rage, part terror, then reeled to one side by instinct. This blind reaction saved his life as a bolt zipped past his throat and thudded into the shoulder of the man behind him.

The wounded man screamed, then something struck Mabon on the side of the head, and he was knocked to the ground. Again, instinct drove his arm out in a hard sweep with the sword still clasped in his fist, but this time, his reply was thwarted by the cold clang of metal on metal. The young man, head still ringing from the blow, registered the agility of the blade that had met his, then realized his father's sword was no longer in his hand.

Reeling back, Mabon saw the svartalf's grinning face an instant before a pointed boot thudded into his face.

The world took on a gel-like quality, as though everything around him was moments from being sealed in amber. His eyes remained opened, but so wild and surreal were the images he saw that his rattled mind assured him he was dreaming. Death came from bolt and blade. Everything moved slowly until he blinked, then the vision leapt to a mound of bodies and merciful thrusts ending his men's suffering.

Mabon's skull throbbed, but he tried to cry out. He wanted to beg for someone to hear him and send help, but his voice would not obey him.

He blinked again, then he saw a boot pressing down on his neck. He followed the boot up the tall figure to a hungry smile.

"Just a moment now, good Captain," the svartalf cooed, red eyes gleaming. "My friends will no doubt have some questions for you once they're done…sorting out your disciplinary issues."

CHAPTER SEVEN

"We don't need a captive," Torbjorn said, pretending he couldn't see the whisker-chinned human staring up at him from beneath Utyrvaul's boot.

"Oh, dear," Utyrvaul remarked with a frown. "Well, this is uncomfortable. I wonder what we shall do with this one, then?"

Raising a finger to his lips, he tapped the flat of his sword on the unfortunate human's head. Torbjorn swiped blood from his sword with a rag, his scowl darkening as he glared at the elf. He knew the answer, and so did Utyrvaul, but no matter how he tried, he couldn't force the words onto his tongue.

"We've got to shift these bodies to that ravine," Torbjorn stated. "Take care of things before I get back."

He nearly choked as the last words came out, but naked necessity drove them. It was mere chance that the lad had twisted away from Torbjorn's shot at the last instant, just the fortunes of war. The boy should already be dead, and Torbjorn couldn't let himself think about this situation any other way. He had enough trouble without dragging around a longshanks who'd give them away at the first opportunity.

"That's quite the quandary you've put me in, Commander."

Utyrvaul sighed. "How will a simple elf like me know what to do without your sage guidance?"

Torbjorn turned his back on the elf, motioning for the three hale dwarfs to help him haul the dead humans toward a ravine they'd passed, where they might remain unnoticed for a little longer.

"Just imagine you swore an oath of loyalty to the boy," Torbjorn replied. "Then do what you normally do in such circumstances."

Utyrvaul's answering laugh set Torbjorn's teeth on edge, but he kept things moving.

Torbjorn set off, and the wounded sank to the ground to rest. The svartalf held his thoughtful conqueror pose for a moment before bending over the human once more. When he spoke, his voice was a whisper the nearby dwarfs could not hear.

"Think quickly, little midge," the elf purred. "Is there any reason for me to keep you alive?"

The human looked childlike, eyes brimming with tears. He tried to speak, but only a coarse croak came out. It took much gulping and grunting to make any headway toward being understood. Through it all, Utyrvaul's blade was close at hand, and his face was inscrutable.

"P-please," the young man wheezed, massaging his throat. "M-my name's Mabon, Mabon Reeve, a-a-and—"

The flat of Utyrvaul's blade tapped the boy smartly on the head, interrupting him.

"Time is of the essence, mayfly," the svartalf warned, his silken voice cold. "You need to provide me with a very good reason not to kill you, or my compatriots, shorter in stature and temper, will wonder why you haven't joined your companions in the bliss of oblivion."

To the surprise of both, when the human next spoke, newfound steel rang in his voice, and his terrified stammer had nearly vanished.

"If you want me to turn on Paelon's Watch, forget it," Mabon declared, glancing fearfully at the blade by his face. "I'm no traitor."

Utyrvaul cocked one eyebrow, his mouth curling into a sneer.

"What a pity. A traitor would be of some use to me," he replied, his sword's point drifting under the young man's chin. "Though I'm not sure what use I would have for Paelon's Watch since your town is nothing to us except in our way."

Mabon's breath caught as naked steel tickled the hollow of his throat. His gaze sharpened at the elf's words. Panicked and conflicting thoughts bounced between his ears.

"You're running?" he murmured, the first fires of hope springing up in his racing mind.

"More like limping at this point," Utyrvaul said, tilting his head at the injured dwarfs. "Some of my compatriots had a hard time passing over your fair mountains, so our progress has been hobbled."

The svartalf could hear the gears of the little mortal's mind whirring as a plan formed.

"At this r-rate, you'll never outrun the wight lord and his a-army," Mabon stated, pausing to make sure he didn't feel the bite of a blade parting his throat. "You need sh-shelter, a place to r-rest."

The point of the sword tilted up, and Mabon's neck strained to keep clear of the cruel tip.

"You wouldn't happen to know of such a place, would you?" Utyrvaul asked, his smile widening.

"You knew about this all along?" Torbjorn asked. He was breathless since it was his turn to help Waelon shuffle forward.

Ahead of the group, Gromic clasped his magsax in one meaty hand and the end of a rope in the other. At the other end was the neck of young Mabon Reeve, who was guiding the Bad Badgers to his family's homestead near the foot of the mountain.

"How did you know?" the dwarf commander pressed. "How *could* you know?"

The svartalf scowled at his sleeve and picked at a crust of dirt that had escaped his notice until then.

"Know? Well, 'know' is too definitive a term," Utyrvaul muttered absently, preening as he walked alongside the dwarf. "I concluded that the poor midge was the sort who might be able to direct us to temporary lodgings away from prying eyes."

Torbjorn frowned as he looked at the pitiful figure shambling along with a rope knotted around his throat—the very throat Torbjorn had intended to put a bolt through.

"Fine, not know." The dwarf commander huffed in irritation. "How did you come to that *conclusion?*"

"Myrkling witchery," Waelon stated, the bitterness in his voice sharpened by pain. "Foul sorcery."

As was his wont, the svartalf met the vitriol with a titter.

"Only if using what's on either side of my nose and between my ears is magic," the elf retorted, giving the big dwarf an appraising look. "In your case, it *would* be a matter of supernatural significance."

Waelon snarled, then gave an agonized gasp as he went to round on the elf.

"Steady on," Torbjorn warned, balancing the fiery-haired dwarf. He turned his attention back to Utyrvaul. "Stop being obtuse and tell me what you so keenly perceived, elf."

His audience's patience was wearing thin. "Well, the first thing I noticed was the sword," he began, one tapered hand coming to rest on his fresh acquisition. "The craftsmanship, even in an heirloom piece, speaks of quality that requires affluence to possess and maintain. I mean, this is mammoth ivory from the steppes to the west."

Torbjorn didn't comment on the elf's vainglorious infatuation with the weapon for fear that it might derail his explanation.

"Next was the midge's age," Utyrvaul continued, stroking the sword hilt affectionately. "I admit I wasn't certain until the creature spoke since most humans look like swollen toddlers to my eyes until they wilt and shrivel, but once I heard the brittle voice of a midge not quite mature leading members of his kind, several of whom were much older, I was almost certain his family was quality, or what passes for it among their kind."

The dwarf commander nodded. He hated that he saw the myrkling's point, even as he chaffed under the superior tone it was delivered in.

"The final bit of evidence, the nail in the proverbial coffin as it were, was the disposition of those serving under him." The elf sighed, a hint of bemused disappointment touching his lilting voice. "Humans are fractious creatures and prone to reject authority, not just when bestowed by something as legitimate as a birthright but especially when that is present. The animosity of his fellow creatures cemented my conviction that he was a youth of means, so his family would most likely have a domicile of agreeable size outside the town."

Torbjorn thought the elf's comments about authority by birthright were odd, given his relationship with his previous leader. The ways of elves being beyond the dwarf's ken, he decided to leave it alone. Another condescending remark after that arch explanation, and Torbjorn might forget himself and put a fist in the myrkling's guts on principle.

Gromic had come to a halt with the point of his magsax against the human's spine. Ahead of them, the path separated into many that wound off in different directions.

"We have to go west," Mabon explained, his voice no less hoarse than when the boot was fresh off his neck. "Down that path three miles, then the way cut through the trees will take us to my home."

The stout dwarf looked over his shoulder at his commander, blue eyes narrowed in suspicion.

"What'd you say, sir?"

Torbjorn would have traced the scar on his cheek if he hadn't been occupied by holding Waelon up. He saw the danger in taking the western path that gradually sloped downhill but also moved them back to the mountain arm they'd shuffled down for hours. Going in that direction might put them in sight of the pursuing wheezer vanguard.

But their pace was growing slower, and if they wouldn't attempt to reach the human's estate, they might as well pitch camp here and wait for the enemy to find them.

"Keep moving." The dwarf commander grunted. "He knows what'll happen if he leads us astray."

Gromic nodded and threw him an exaggerated wink, then leaned forward to growl at Mabon's back.

"Hear that, longshanks? You play us foul, and I'll cut you so that it'll take you days to die."

As the lad gulped affirmation past the rope at his throat, Gromic looked over his shoulder for approval at his theatrics. Mindful of keeping the squad's spirits up, Torbjorn managed a grim nod of approval before setting his shoulder to the task of hauling Waelon the three more miles they had to go.

CHAPTER EIGHT

"This...is not what I expected."

The disappointed frown puckering the svartalf's face made Mabon nervous, but it was nothing compared to the smoldering scowls on the dwarven faces. Even the red-haired dwarf he'd heard called Waelon, who winced and gasped with every step, had enough heart left to offer a reviling curse.

"Thieving, murderous bastards, every one of them."

Grunts of affirmation rose from every dwarf, and none more so than the two younger troops. Mabon fought the urge to tug on the rope about his neck when he gulped as their gazes fell on him.

"This isn't an estate," the sister spat.

"It's a homestead," her brother said. "A dwarvish homestead."

Mabon wanted to argue that although dwarfs had once lived in the stout building constructed of stone and timber, it didn't mean it was forever and always the property of the doughty people who had built it. If he could have unstuck his dry and swollen tongue, he might have asked them if they found a gold coin lying on the road with no soul in sight, wouldn't they put it in their pocket to put toward feeding their family?

He was certain that all the rational arguments in the world would do him no good. Instead, he had to focus on making sure everyone within the homestead made it through this encounter alive. Mabon thought he too would like to survive this encounter if the Watchman could spare the goodwill for that.

The leader traded places with the immense dwarf who'd been trudging at Mabon's back. His dark beard bristled with indignation at being this close to a human. When he spoke, his voice was like rocks being ground together.

"Who's at home?" he asked, winding the end of the rope around his fist.

A sudden and urgent desire to lie came over Mabon. He felt like a child caught in the midst of tomfoolery.

"I don't know. I was called up by the magistrate last night, and I haven't been home since." It was true, but he couldn't keep his eyes from scanning the yard and the outbuildings.

The darting glances didn't escape the dwarf's notice, and he kept looping the rope around his hand.

"Who are you looking for?"

Mabon again felt the urge to lie, but when his gaze met the eyes of the other dwarfs, he knew that his life and the lives of every other soul here would depend on the honesty of his words.

"Dillon, our manservant, and his son Kai," the young man said. "They'd usually be out splitting wood at this time, but they must have headed into town since they aren't."

Mabon's hand shook as he pointed at the stout stump set in earth, which was coated with a fine blanket of wood slivers. Behind stood a deep-bellied woodshed with dwarvish runes carved into its frame, evoking the warmth of the deep earth and driving away pestilential damp.

"Looks like you're a fair bit behind on wood," the dwarf commander observed. "Where would your servant be if your home is so poorly prepared for the winter?"

As though on cue, a sharp wind rushed down from the

mountains, carrying a thin flurry of snow. Mabon shivered, his mind racing to find an answer that would allay the dwarf's suspicions.

"I don't know," he admitted, feeling every dwarf's eyes on him. "Dillon has a crooked leg from...well, from serving as an irregular under the wights. With the weather changing, my mother might have sent him on an errand to town rather than having him aching in the yard and not getting much done."

The dwarf commander nodded and let go of the length of rope he'd just begun to wrap around his fist.

"Where's your father?"

The young man couldn't explain why he was embarrassed, but it took him another breath or two to force the answer out.

"Dead five years ago," he said, refusing to look down at his feet as he spoke despite the burning in his cheeks.

"How?" the dwarf leader asked.

"Was the bailiff for the magistrate, chosen to hunt down some bandits," Mabon told him. "Except they weren't bandits but dwarvish rangers raiding past the Pickets. Took a bolt in the chest but made it back home to die of the blood-fever five days later."

As he finished recounting the tale, his eyes roved across his captors. The elf and several of the dwarfs had expressions that were at best inscrutable if not mildly hostile, while the young dwarf siblings looked as though they were unsatisfied by his explanation.

Probably think it was too quick, Mabon thought, then winced as he recalled the last fever-addled hours of his father's life stretching on. *I would not wish that on anyone.*

When his gaze returned to the dwarf leader, Mabon was unprepared for what he saw.

Was that pity on the dwarf's rough-hewn features? Was the glistening in his eyes more than just the sting of the wind?

"Sorry about that, lad," he remarked, then grunted to clear his throat. "I assume your mother's in the house, then. Any other servants, or maybe a sibling or two?"

"Should be," Mabon answered, bemusement softening his words as he shot the dwarf a sidelong glance. "That is, my mother, brother, and sister should be, in along with Dillon's woman Betrys. Unless any of them went to town with Dillon."

The dwarf nodded again and went back to eyeing the house and barn tucked behind a row of fruit-bearing trees.

"Any beasts about?" the leader asked. "Dogs, swine, horses, the like?"

Mabon's jaw tightened. He was uncertain how he should answer.

"Understand this, lad," the dark-eyed dwarf began. "I've no interest in pillaging your home or giving your kin more trouble than is absolutely necessary, but I'm going to take any surprise as a threat and act accordingly. So, if you have any living things in your home, barn, or elsewhere that you want to keep breathing, you tell me now. Otherwise, I make no promises for their safety."

Mabon searched the dwarf's face, and like something he hadn't understood had pulled him out of the way of that bolt on the mountain path, something confirmed that the dwarf leader was trustworthy.

Watchman, spare this fool, he prayed before forcing another swallow.

"Dillon would've taken our plow horse Lloyd to pull the wagon," the young man said. "My mother's mare is also there with her foal, but please don't hurt them. The mare is the last gift my father ever gave my mother and is very precious to her. Well, to all of us."

The dwarf looked at the barn, then glanced over his shoulder at the svartalf and jerked his head toward the structure.

"Have a quiet peek while we go introduce ourselves, but leave the beasts alone. You find anyone hiding in there, give a shout before you run 'em through with your pretty new sword."

The leader of the ragged band pointed at the front door of Mabon's home.

"Time to go in, lad."

Torbjorn bid the wounded and Haeda and the girl to stay at the edge of the yard. The rest advanced to the front door with their captive. The commander had quietly slid the broad-bladed sword from his belt and was pleased to see that Gromic and Ober had their duabuws in hand and primed. They had barely a handful of bolts between them, which wasn't comforting, but if this wasn't a masterfully executed trap, it would be more than enough.

And if it was a trap? Well, a few more bolts wouldn't make any difference.

Dwarfs and human stood before the door. Its frame had been modified to accommodate taller occupants than those who had built the place. The rough alterations were an affront to any dwarf for their crudeness, but to see them on a former homestead screamed a reminder of what had taken place here. On the commander's left, he heard a choked bestial snarl slip between Ober's lips.

Going to have to keep an eye on those two, he reminded himself as he motioned for Mabon to knock on the front door. *Assuming we aren't immediately found out.*

The young man's trembling hand faltered long enough that Torbjorn's hand tightened on the hilt of his magsax, then he pressed on the door but found it locked. His face drained of color at the unexpected impediment. The dwarf commander thrust his chin at the door, and the human rapped smartly on the timber portal.

There was movement within, and an indistinct exchange of feminine voices. One moved closer to the door, and its words became distinguishable to Torbjorn's straining ears.

"Sure one of them just forgot something," declared the young, confident voice of a lass who couldn't have been far from maturity but was not there yet. "I promise if it's a troll, I'll tell it no one's home."

The door opened with a rush of warmth and the tittering of women. On the delicate features of a young female, a bright smile formed.

"What did you forget, si—" the lass began. Her voice faltered when she saw the state of her brother and the naked dwarvish steel.

"Cerys, don't scream," Mabon wheezed, his hands raised in placation. "You need to stay calm."

Her rosy cheeks paled as her lips pressed into a grim line. Her hands fell from the door to ball into fists on her narrow hips. Her hazel eyes flashed with a spirit Torbjorn found admirable as Cerys gave him a once over. She turned the same scrutinizing eye upon Gromic and Ober, who were a few steps behind.

"What is the meaning of this?" the young woman demanded, her voice carrying an authority at odds with her round, cherubic face.

"Cerys, please," her brother begged, advancing a half-step before Torbjorn checked him with a tug of the rope. "Stay calm."

"Cerys, what's going on?" came an age-deepened voice that carried the same sharp authority as Mabon's sister. "Who's at the door?"

"Bandits, mother," Cerys replied tersely over her shoulder. "And not properly sized ones at that. It seems we don't get anything but stunted brigands."

"Oh, you and your tongue girl," the elder Reeve called. "If only etiquette came as quick as fibs and sass from that mouth."

"No fibs and no sass, Mother," the lass called back, holding the dwarven commander's eye. "Just a pungent pack of badgers."

Mabon looked at Torbjorn in horror. He could see that the lad was trying to decide whether to beg for his sister's life or throw himself in front of her. As an answer, Torbjorn gave an amused snort as he met Cerys' flashing eye with a burning stare.

"Perhaps I ought to be talking to your mother, lass," the dwarf suggested and drew the rope lower so her brother bowed. "Mabon assured us we could find hospitality here. Only temporary, I assure you."

Cerys made to open her mouth. Torbjorn was sure she was going to tell him where he could put her brother's assurances, but a set of long, square fingers seized her shoulder and dragged her away.

In her place stood a tall, handsome woman who alternated between pained looks at her eldest son and imperious looks at the armed dwarfs.

"What is the meaning of this?" she demanded, her voice stronger yet more brittle than her daughter's. "Why are you here, and what have you done to my son?"

"What we did was spare your son's life," Torbjorn stated, offering a flat smile. "And in return, he offered his home as a place of respite, long enough for our wounded to recover. It seemed that he thought it a better offer than the business we finished with his compatriots."

Mabon's face fell, and his mother's mouth tightened to a thin, bloodless line.

"Now, unless you'd like to contest that negotiation," Torbjorn said, planting one foot across the threshold as the woman retreated half a step, "may we enter your lovely home?"

CHAPTER NINE

"We should put a bolt in each of them and be done with it."

Haeda looked sharply at Tomza from where she was settling the girl down to nap. As was standard for most dwarvish homes, the ground floor was a single large room with a central open-sided hearth, while beneath that, the house was portioned into four rooms framed in stone that acted as bedrooms. A cursory look around the current room suggested it was Cerys'. The thin but vibrantly colored fabrics over the lanterns cast the area in a kaleidoscope of colors that suggested that for all her ferocity, the human was very much still a child.

Unfortunately, that did nothing to soften Tomza's venomous mood. Haeda found herself more than a little put off. She shushed the girl, running fingers through her blue-black hair while thinking about what to say to Tomza.

"So, we're for killing children and housewives then?" the older dwarfess finally asked, unable to hide her distaste at the thought. "I thought you and your brother needed salting when you first joined up, but I take it back. You're salty enough that I think I might choke."

The driver met the younger dwarfess' eyes and was shocked

to see defiance at the rebuke. Not defiance, but something hotter and sharper. Haeda wondered if she'd always known that hidden, jagged edge to the lass was there. It had given her pause from the moment she'd first set eyes on Tomza. When the revelation of witchery had emerged, Haeda had told herself it was that, but now seeing it bared and ugly in the clashing colors of the lantern light, she knew it was more.

Stone knows I've got pains, but something in this lass…

Haeda remembered that Tomza and Ober were Valeborn, and the first piece fell into place.

"They're not the ones who took your home, lass," Haeda stated softly, stroking the girl's hair. "They might bear a passing resemblance to them, but they're not, and you have to remember that if you're going to keep your head through this."

Tomza's laugh cut the air sharply enough that the girl jumped and stirred in Haeda's arms before nestling back down, one hand covering her ear.

"You're talking like they're innocent," Tomza snarled. "They might not have taken my home, but they took someone's, and every single *minute* they've spent here has been a theft of a good dwarf's sweat, tears, and blood. They probably had the clackers do their dirty work, slaughtering the owners or driving them out, but these spindle-legged scum don't even have the excuse of undeath to justify their murderous theft!"

The power of Tomza's fury caught Haeda by surprise and might have otherwise staggered her into silence for some time. Yet, she felt the human girl trembling, understanding the cutting intensity of the words if not their intention. The child's fear woke an icy fire in Haeda that showed in her emerald eyes as she regarded Tomza coolly.

"Get control of yourself, Dwan," she retorted with a frosty evenness to her tone. "We are in far too tight a spot for you to come apart, hurt or not. Now get control of yourself, or I'll find a way to settle that tongue for you."

Tomza's eyes flashed and her mouth opened for another violent response when she caught the golden eyes, wide and frightened, watching her from beneath the driver's stout arm. Tomza's mouth shut so smartly that her teeth gave an audible clack and she winced.

Haeda was willing to bet the lass' reaction had nothing to do with her teeth hurting, and that realization left her feeling an aching sympathy that she would not allow to reach her face.

"I get it. Your home was taken from you, and probably much worse than that," the driver pressed, her voice lowering without losing any of its intensity. "But we're here, outside of Paelon's Watch, with a whole bloody army on our tail and two dwan too battered to make a run for the Pickets. The only thing keeping us alive is laying low until you're recovered enough to witch yourself and Waelon back to fighting fit, and that means being smart and quiet."

Tomza's eyes drifted from the older dwarfess to her propped-up ankle in its swaddling of stabilizing bandages. The fire in her eyes died, banked behind the edge that still gleamed there in a more controlled manner. When she finally spoke, it was in a low, rasping tone.

"I'm not going to do anything stupid," she said. "Besides, I'm not sure I could even if I wanted to."

Haeda relaxed when she felt the hard lines going out of the girl pressed to her side, but she refused to let Tomza's eyes escape her gaze.

"That's where you're wrong, lass," she warned. "Those longshanks, however monstrous you think 'em, are scared. The head of their family's dead, and the boy who's been trying to fill those shoes showed up with a rope around his neck and a band of angry dwans holding the other end. They're terrified, and the only thing keeping them compliant is them thinking that we're reasonable and predictable. One of them hears you talking like that, and suddenly they've got nothing left to lose by plotting against us. Can't get much rest if you're always sleeping with one eye open, you follow?"

One look confirmed that Tomza did understand, but then a searching, suspicious narrowness came over her expression.

"Sounds like you've done this sort of thing before," she observed, one eyebrow rising in question.

Haeda felt the child's breathing even out but she held her position, still idly stroking the child's hair. Occasionally, her strong, sure fingers would find a knot or a tangle to expertly unravel before continuing the tidal repetition of hand over indigo-streaked tresses.

"One of my first operations with the Bad Badgers," Haeda began, "we were sent to try to find a savageling pirate moving along the Wesvon River and see if an agreement could be reached. Turns out the enemy of my enemy isn't always enough, though. Poor intelligence about the situation and some unlikely accidents saw us going to ground in Adaelton. You ever been there?"

Tomza shook her head and adjusted herself into a more comfortable position. The anger burning at the back of her throat wasn't gone, but Haeda's husky voice was soothing, and the young dwarfess was beyond exhausted.

"Adaelton's not on the Wesvon, but it is along a tributary that eventually reconnects with the Blue Wyrm," she explained, fingers picking expertly at a stubborn knot. "Despite this, it's a river town, so it had plenty of seedy places along the docks where we could hunker down and lick our wounds. We numbered closer to a dozen when we set out, but by the time we settled into a rundown warehouse, we were half that number. Should've been an easy thing, squatting among the rotting crates with everything stinking of fish, but like I said, that operation was choked with unlikely accidents."

Tomza felt her eyes drooping and every bone sinking lower in her body. There was a relief in the settling. Fingers she hadn't realized she'd been clenching slid into her lap as the driver continued her tale.

"A batch of humans, vagabonds, had been using the place, seeing much the same value as we did. Half of us were sleeping when they slipped in, but we all roused quick enough when their little boy gave a shriek at Jorm's ugly mug peeking up from between the crates. Jorm tried clapping a hand to the lad's mouth, but his mother, just being a good parent, sprang in with a knife and buried it to the hilt in Jorm's throat. Now, Jorm wasn't well-liked and probably deserved worse than a quick, clean end like that, but a scream, the sight of steel, and a dead dwan all in the blink of an eye? Well, it wasn't going to end well."

Tomza was nodding off and accepted it, her head bobbing lower as Haeda's words rolled over her. Turn about being fair play, the older dwarfess had stopped caring if her junior was listening.

"By the time things had settled enough for anyone to tell what had happened, the woman was dead, and the little human was on his way. The father got to hold the poor lad for the last moments, along with his daughter, who looked a few years older. Torbjorn let them have that moment, then tied them up with apologies that none of this was what we wanted. I remember seeing the man's eyes as we tied him up. We were murderers and monsters to him, the ones who'd taken his love and his baby boy from him. He didn't trust us, and he was going to fight us at every turn."

Haeda's words were met by the droning breath of both child and dwarfess, but the weight of the story dragged the end from her lips. It was a story that had to be finished once started.

"Two nights later, when we were untying them so they could ease their limbs and eat something, they made their move. Without waiting for their hands to be undone, the man attacked, and the girl made to flee. Man almost got a magsax before a bolt took him through the heart. The girl leapt out a window that overlooked the tributary. Water was deeper than she expected, and with her hands bound and clothes wet, she made it far enough to draw attention to our hiding spot before she sank."

Haeda's hand finally stopped petting the girl, unshed tears shining in her eyes.

"Too bad nobody thought to fish her out before they came after us."

"When will they be back?" Torbjorn asked. He alternated between looking through the ground floor's narrow shutters and regarding Crysten Reeve, Mabon's mother.

"I don't know," she replied, standing before the hearth as though refusing to surrender full control of her home to interlopers. "Tell me when you plan to leave my home."

"Funny," Gromic rumbled without humor as he adjusted his grip on his duabuw, his eyes never leaving the approach through the trees. "When we took your boy, he seemed to think this place was his."

The dwarvish commander didn't appreciate the stout dwarf antagonizing their captives, but he let it slide. Gromic, like all of them, was tired, hungry, and still faced with the reality that death could march their way at any moment. Snark was the least of their concerns, but Mabon's mother was not in nearly as tolerant a mood.

"Mabon is the man of the house, but I am mistress here," she shot back sharply. "And as the mistress, I demand to know how much longer my family must tolerate this intrusion?"

Her flashing glare rankled Torbjorn as much as her tone, but he forced himself to swallow the snarled retort of "As long as I damn well say so!" His temper was not what it should be, but he was wise enough to know the short-term pleasure of a vented spleen would cost him more of the human's goodwill than he cared to tolerate.

"No longer than necessary, you have my word," he replied. "The moment I can move my dwans out, I will gladly do so, but in the meantime, I'm afraid you will have to tolerate a few uninvited guests."

"I imagine this is the part where you are going to voice your protests again," Utyrvaul spoke from where he stood watching the rear windows. "I'm sure that this time, they will be far more convincing than the last three times you did."

"That'll do, Utyrvaul," Torbjorn replied curtly, making a short bow to the lady of the house. "Please, excuse the myrkling. His idea of manners is…peculiar."

The dwarf commander's efforts were met with as much disdain as Utyrvaul's taunts. The woman's lips tightened into a hard line through which ground-out words escaped with mangled fury.

"As peculiar as dwarfs thinking a soft word will have me forget they are pointing one of their fiendish crossbows at my second son after beating and throttling my eldest with a rope. It seems what passes for manners is peculiar among all your barbaric kind!"

"Mother, please," Mabon groaned, raising a hand to halt his sisters' ministrations to his battered head. Most of the blood had been dabbed away, and the young woman's hands were poised to take needle and thread to the split skin. At her side, the servant Betrys gathered the bloodied rags into a basket. The graying woman had not said a word since the dwarfs had entered, but her cheeks glittered with quiet, frightened tears.

"No, Mabon. This is my house, and I will have my say!" Crysten cried, her voice rising so sharply that Torbjorn almost raised a hand to shield his ears. "This is our home, and these… these brutes have no right to be here!"

Torbjorn's ire rose, a bubbling heat at the back of his tongue that warmed his mouth with fiery recriminations. He swallowed most of it as he turned back to peer through the shutters, but the distraction of the movement was enough to let a few hot words hop off his tongue.

"I'm sure the dwarfs who built this home would say the same, Mistress Reeve," he observed, one thumb tracing the line of his scarred cheek before he rested his hand on a rune-graven stone set into the wall. "That assumes their bones aren't scattered across these woods, picked apart by whatever beasts fetched them from a shallow grave."

The answer to Torbjorn's words was a silence he had not expected. It intrigued him enough to swing his eyes back to the woman standing before the stolen hearth. She was shaking with rage and humiliation, yet suddenly mute. Torbjorn might have offered a crooked smile at her silence if he'd not been so tired and sick with the acknowledgment of what he'd said. He heard Gromic growl at his spoken truth, but Torbjorn couldn't even manage that. Instead, he stared into the pale blue eyes of the Reeve matron. After a heartbeat and then another, the woman looked away, beaten.

"It's not our fault the dwarfs woke the wights," Cerys began. "It wasn't humans who walked into their tombs, too greedy to listen to the warnings of the woselings."

"The darling midge does have a point." Utyrvaul snickered. "Not that I'm taking a side, mind you. My people have minded the words our wild cousins gibbered for near on three millennia if the tales are to be believed."

"The doom-speaking of the savagelings was as reliable as a loincloth in a windstorm," Torbjorn retorted. "If we'd believed them, our forces would have slunk back to Torvgrud to await our inevitable end when the Crow Prince came to eat our eyes and livers one and all. And none of that matters when considering that the undead rose and every human in the Vale seemed quite happy to come out of the south from as far as Aruhkham and the steppes to serve them for the promise of land to be had on the bones of honest dwarfs."

"There are bad dwarfs for sure," Gromic interjected. "But not a one has ever bent his knee to a wheezer. The living were not meant to serve the dead."

Cerys was ready to argue despite her brother's pleading look and her mother's continued silence, but Torbjorn raised his fist for quiet. The rumble of wagon wheels on rutted ground carried through the air. Squinting through the slats, he could just make out the lumpy figure of a wagon wobbling down the track.

Torbjorn gave three heavy stomps of his foot, then eyed the humans in the open room.

"Listen very carefully," he said, his gaze finding each human face. "We'll need them all to come inside so the situation can be explained. Cooperate and no one will be hurt, and this will be over that much quicker."

As the commander spoke, Ober and Haeda emerged with duabuws in hand. They looked at Torbjorn and then the humans, ready and waiting.

"Raise the alarm, incite a struggle, or do anything remotely foolish, and someone in your family is going to die," the dwarf leader continued. "I do not want that to happen, but I am sincerely asking you not to test my resolve. My dwans have been instructed to give no quarter and kill any who try to escape."

"I've been instructed to shoot your son from the jump," Gromic added, his eyes fixed on the approaching wagon. "Remember that before you get any smart ideas."

Torbjorn stifled a wince. He felt like reminding the stout dwarf what he had told him about improvising for effect, which was *not* to. One look at the Reeve matron told Torbjorn that she understood and needed no further coaxing. Human faces were so exaggeratedly expressive as to be confusing if not grotesque to most dwarfs, but the slackness in her expression was easy for him to read. She was cowed for the moment, though he was not fool enough to believe it was a permanent state of affairs.

"You will invite them in for a midday meal, and we'll have a talk with them," Torbjorn explained. "Simple as that. Understand?"

The woman nodded, then looked at her son and daughter and held the gaze of the latter until she gave a stiff nod of assent. The shame-faced Mabon bobbed his head once, then contemplated the floor.

Have to watch that one. Only so long before he does something really stupid.

Right now, everything in the lad's posture spoke of dejected surrender, and Torbjorn would gladly take it.

The wagon was in the yard, and three human males climbed down as they chattered and joked. Their breath fogged in the chill, which had not surrendered any ground since the night, and all three had apple-red cheeks and shining noses.

Torbjorn tried not to imagine all three lying on the frosted earth, especially the smallest, who looked to be little older than the girl.

His eyes swung back to Crysten Reeve, hoping that by sheer will, his stare would force her to cooperate.

Still the same slack expression, but had he judged wrongly? Was it surrender or a ploy?

Stone help us.

Taking a breath, he nodded and motioned the woman to the door.

CHAPTER TEN

"That could have been much worse."

Gromic's evaluation wasn't wrong, but Ober was nursing a lumpy jaw while chewing a piece of mona root, and he did not share the stout dwarf's optimism.

"That's too tight," the human at his feet groaned as Ober tightened the last of the knots that bound every man hand to foot and to one another. "I can't feel my fingers."

Ober looked at the leathery creature issuing the complaint, the manservant of the Reeve family, who was hunched next to his shivering son. Under normal circumstances, he might have felt something for the man, bound and battered as he was and humiliated next to his terrified offspring. However, the lopsided configuration had come when the human had thought to hurl a stool at his head. The young dwarf had twisted to one side, resulting in a glancing blow, but it still had left him with a misshapen jaw and a foul temper.

"Jusht imagine 'ow 'at bothersh me," he slurred through his swollen mouth. "You're lucky to be feeling anything, dhough. By all rightsh, you should be dhead. Thank your son for that mercy."

Dillon's eyes narrowed, and his gaze darted to his son.

Whether by dumb luck or due to the grizzled manservant's twisted leg, the scrappy old battler had lost his footing in his ill-conceived attack and fallen flat as Ober had reeled, clutching his jaw. Dwarvish crossbows had swung to target the prone man, and Kai, his son, had lunged forward to cover his father with his body. For one long heartbeat, every armed dwarf was perched on a precipice they knew would descend into bloodshed. Fortunately, Torbjorn had told them to stay their hands.

Ober, his temper flaring, might not have listened as he muttered curses from behind the hand nursing his jaw, but even in his indignation, he would not have wanted the boy to die. Dillon had been warned against taking action when he'd limped into the house at Crysten's invitation. If things had been different, it would have only been fair to put the fool down, but his son? Well, even as the injured party, he could not demand that recompense.

The young dwarf remembered a time at another dwarf homestead when he'd thrown himself in the way to spare his felled father. It had not been effective in his case, but he could recall the impulse.

He felt the other presence within him stir, the primal spirit unmoved by the display and eager to vent its growing ire. Ober had felt the prickle of fur beginning to press through his flesh. It was only desperation-honed habits that had seen his hand go for the mona root. Jaw throbbing with the effort, he ground the fibrous tuber between his teeth and the juice ran down his throat, drowning the growing bestial growl that heralded a savage eruption.

Close. Too close, he told himself as he chewed.

Being tired is no excuse for letting it get that close.

"Come on, lad," Gromic called, settling a massive paw on Ober's back. "We'll lock this lot in for the night, then see about some food."

Ober looked at him and pointed incredulously at the egg-sized malformation purpling the side of his jaw.

"What?" Gromic asked. "Oh, you mean your jaw. Who knows, maybe Haeda's made soup? Not that it will taste any better than her other cooking, but you could eat it. Can't complain about that, can you?"

Ober could, but his jaw was aching even more than before, and he decided he'd spare his companion the muttered and likely incomprehensible reply.

Torbjorn sat at the foot of the stairs, duabuw across his lap, fighting to keep his burning eyes open.

He'd insisted the others eat and sleep while he took first watch. For a time, it had eased his weariness to listen to them move around above him. He heard them mutter and shuffle, too tired and strained for much in the way of the usual dwarvish boisterousness. He still heard the odd curse or low chuckle, and at one point, Utyrvaul had sung a few songs in his tongue before the sounds of snoring had driven him to silence. Torbjorn had popped his head into the ground floor to see dwarfs asleep on tables, in corners, or on the floor. The myrkling was resting against the far wall, his eyelids aflutter with his elvish dreams, seeming for all the world as though he would spring up at the slightest sound.

After checking to make sure the door was latched and bolted, Torbjorn had slunk back down the stairs to watch.

He'd occupied himself by straining his ears to hear if the humans were speaking among themselves. He heard only silence and some truly barbarous snoring from Gromic. There was nothing to do but wait and watch.

Time rolled on, and fatigue threatened to drag him down. Torbjorn tried to think of something to occupy his mind.

Not a soul groused when the elf sang tonight, he observed, then his mouth hitched up in a crooked grin. *Though Waelon being tucked away down here probably helped with that.*

With the exception of Waelon, the dwarfs had to admit the svartalf's voice was a unique pleasure if an acquired taste that they'd grown to appreciate over the days of weary travel. Not as robust and stirring as dwarvish singing, but it had a melancholy and longing that any dwarf, especially one far from home, could sympathize with.

We are a people filled with a longing so deep you could almost call us empty.

Torbjorn smirked as he remembered his old tutor's words.

Born with a desire to save Erduna, yet easily distracted, even though we know it will never be enough. Will never satisfy. A dwarf's soul is an unfathomable void into which he can cast all the gold, jewels, ale, iron, and blood in this world, only to find he's thrown himself away. It is a king's duty to know his people, Torbjorn, so you must understand this about our kind if you are to—

"You look as though you are struggling to make up your mind," stated a soft voice behind Torbjorn. "Either take the step or don't, but loitering on the edge seems hazardous."

He whirled, crossbow rising to his shoulder as his weariness-wasted brain feebly protested that it was only the svartalf. Torbjorn looked up to see Utyrvaul stretched out on the stairs behind him. His stomach twisted when he realized how close the elf had gotten without him noticing.

A sentry asleep on his feet gets dwans killed as surely as one in his bed.

"You come to relieve me, elf?" Torbjorn asked. "Or did you have a bad dream and need me to tuck you back in?"

Utyrvaul smirked, but there was no laughter or twittering giggle. Either the elf was still out of sorts from having just woken up from his nap, or he didn't appreciate the mocking simper he so often used being turned on him. Torbjorn couldn't help wishing for more of the latter than the former since it would aid him in sorting out the slippery elf in the future.

"You'd trust me to keep watch alone?" Utyrvaul asked. "This is the first time you've ever placed that much trust in me, Commander. I imagine this pleasant turn of events has to do with your little test when we first arrived."

Torbjorn frowned at the reclining myrkling, his incomprehension stoking a flame of irritation that put heat in his retort.

"What in the Deep are you talking about?"

The svartalf's smile didn't waver, although his eyes narrowed.

"I can't tell if you are being coy or you are just so tired you don't remember," the elf mused. "The bit of theater with the barn when we first approached. If ever I wanted a chance to cut my losses and flee, it would have been when you sent me to a barn where we expected to find a fine riding horse, yes?"

Torbjorn's brows knotted as he tried to match his memory of events with the duplicitous machinations the svartalf had clearly considered.

"You think I sent you to the barn by yourself as a test?"

Utyrvaul was caught by surprise, and the departure of his unctuous charm was a chilling sight. The myrkling's eyes glittered with a flat, naked hunger, a serpentine intelligence staring at the dwarf commander. The elf's head slid to one side as the long, supple neck bunched. Torbjorn was sure he'd seen the same movements on a viper considering a strike.

"So, you're saying it wasn't a test?"

The dwarf shook his shaggy head and leaned on the stout timbers framing the stairs.

"Utyrvaul, you've had more than enough chances to betray us." Torbjorn sighed. "When we've been at camp, when I needed you to spy out the gremalkins, when I sent you to fetch Tomza and Ober, and yes, when we met with the human patrol. The truth is that I've been at your mercy often enough that I've come to accept that it is worth the risk. I'm past trying to guess your loyalties since we left the shadow of the Tooth."

The cold-blooded evaluation continued for a moment longer, then the mask reappeared.

"Careful, Commander," the elf chided, his cloying smile in place. "It sounds like you see me as part of your little company, as though an elf and a dwarf could do more than just tolerate one another. What a dangerous notion that would be!"

Torbjorn allowed a bark of laughter to pass his lips, then raised a hand to his mouth after grunts and snuffles came from the dwarfs sleeping upstairs.

"Dangerous for both of us, I imagine," Torbjorn said. "Now, are you going to relieve me from my watch or just waste your time to rest being paranoid?"

Utyrvaul stretched his long limbs slowly, letting a long sigh of relief slide between his pointed teeth before throwing a jaunty wink at the dwarf commander.

"Well, I don't think I could catch another wink, knowing my commander is so weary."

With the irritating grace only an elf could muster, he rose fluidly to his feet and threw up a flourishing salute.

"Sir Utyrvaul Urivianoc, here to relieve you, sir."

Torbjorn, chuckling despite himself, returned the salute before staggering upstairs to promptly fall asleep on the floor.

CHAPTER ELEVEN

"All right, where are we as far as the witchery goes?"

It was a sentence that Torbjorn, in all his hard and often obscene days, had never expected to utter. Men were ignorant, infantile heathens and could be excused for their esoteric dabbling, and elves were born with the fiendish stuff, so one could not expect them to avoid it. Dwarfs were supposed to be different. Some outcaste clans had scattered, and the dwarf commander expected they had taken to magic. Then there were the Wain dwarfs—heretics, vagabonds, and feckless sorts who created charms and tokens in a debased sort of mysticism. True dwarfs—Stone-loving, ancestor-honoring, Erduna-restoring dwarfs—knew better than to have anything to do with it.

Yet here he was, a true dwarf, asking a dwarfess under his command to engage in witchery. If he'd had more than a few hours' sleep and time to think, he would probably not do so.

He had neither of those, but he had a job to do, so he waited eagerly for Tomza's reply.

"I think I'm recovered enough to make the attempt," she declared gamely, sitting up straighter against the stone wall. "I'll need to gather some herbs and fresh water from a spring, stream, or river. Has to be fresh moving water."

Herbs and running water. Torbjorn groaned. *Like something out of the storybooks.*

"Could Ober collect what you need?" he asked, noting that while she did look markedly better, her face was still drawn. "You still need to rest, and besides, with that ankle, you'll not be going anywhere fast."

"I think he could manage," she said, nodding after a moment's consideration. "I'll need parchment or the like to make a list and notes about where to look for what I need. Otherwise, he might spend a day without much to show for it. Winter setting in means a fair share of what I require won't be easy to come by."

"That's settled easily enough," Torbjorn said. "It seems that at least the masters of the house are lettered folk unless they keep books only for appearances, so they should have something that will suit our purposes."

Torbjorn noted the tension in the ascedwan's expression at the mention of the humans but decided against addressing the matter at the moment. Tomza was relegated to this room until her leg was healed, so her animosity toward the humans was not a priority. Her brother, on the other hand, would require some checking, especially after the blow his jaw had taken.

"I'll see that you're brought what you need," Torbjorn promised as he headed for the door. "In the meantime, try to rest. We need you to work your craft and be ready to move should trouble find us."

Tomza bobbed her head as she shuffled on the bed where she sat.

"I'll try, sir," she promised with a solemn salute. Her commander returned it before stepping from the room to the narrow hallway that connected the lower rooms to the ground floor.

"Gromic," Torbjorn called and was rewarded a moment later

with the stout dwarf's heavy footfalls as he came thundering down the stairs.

"Yes, sir?" he asked as he approached, one hand raised to swipe the remains of his breakfast from his thick blond beard.

"Tomza needs something to write with and on," Torbjorn explained, moving toward the door leading to the room where they'd stashed Waelon to get some rest. "See that she gets them, then send Ober down to receive instructions."

"Right. Very good, sir," the thick-set dwarf declared as he turned to set to his task. He paused. "Where might I find said writing materials, sir?"

Torbjorn, his hand on the latch to Waelon's temporary room, looked at his former fordwan, then nodded toward the two rooms where the human prisoners were being kept.

"I'd start by asking the lady of the house," he suggested. "She seems to be the sort who believes in a place for everything and everything in its place."

Gromic nodded, then coughed.

"Right. And if she doesn't cooperate, Tweldwan, what then?"

The question hung in the air, Torbjorn refusing to move so much as a mustache whisker as he met the stout dwarf's twinkling blue eyes.

"What are you asking me, Gromic?"

Not for the first time, the immense dwarf's cheeks reddened. He seemed much younger as his eyes darted around for an answer to the question.

"Well, Tweldwan, I'm just never sure about these sorts of situations," he admitted. "If an enemy's coming for me or one of the crew, I put them down cold, no problem. I understand that. Or if an enemy's surrendered and is no longer a threat, I treat them squarely but smartly. I get that too. But this? Well, this doesn't fit into either spot, does it, sir? Like that time in Adaelton."

Torbjorn knew the name of the river town would come up, so he'd braced himself to avoid wincing. He felt the stab in his heart, though. It was a rare week when he didn't remember that young lass' splashing turning into floundering bubbles, or that man holding his son in his arms. The dwarf commander had thought himself beyond redemption before that day, but Adaelton had convinced him of that beyond a shadow of a doubt.

"Do you feel that Madame Reeve, tied up as she is, poses a threat?" he asked.

"Well, not directly, sir, but if she refuses to tell me, that costs us time, see? The more time we're here, the more likely we are to get caught. Getting caught means we're as good as dead and the mission's a failure, so that's sort of a threat, isn't it? And if they're a threat, I'm justified in using what means I have to deal with the situation."

Torbjorn raised a hand to press his eyeballs since the pressure on them increased with every word the former fordwan spoke.

"Yes, I see your point," Torbjorn began, but Gromic wasn't quite done.

"But that's only usually with soldiers, not some poor longshanks lass justly mad about some dwarfs stomping around her home. True, her home is a place her people took from dwarfs when the wights came through, but I'm not sure that has any bearing on this, though given the way Ober and Tomza are talking, it does. Being Valeborn, I'm not sure they don't have confused motives on that count, but the way that Dillon fellow went after Ober, none of them would mind seeing us dangle from a rope."

The dwarf commander looked beseechingly at the stout dwarf, and after taking a pensive breath, Gromic came to his conclusion.

"I'm asking, sir, are they enemies or just unlucky folk we've got to keep shut up for a while?"

This was the question Torbjorn had batted about ever since Utyrvaul's mad scheme had set them on this path. As a professional soldier, he was convinced that prisoners, once taken, had a right to expect a certain civility, but being behind enemy lines changed things. Usually, he was sober-minded enough to say location didn't change the morals, but when the location changed the power dynamics, it would be obtuse to pretend otherwise.

For the moment, Tomza needed something to write on, and he'd made enough moral compromises.

"Go to the lad we caught. Mabon," Torbjorn instructed, feeling a guilty sense of relief as he said the lad's name. "He's a soldier and surrendered readily enough, so I expect he'll cooperate. If not, tell him we'll have to search on our own, and we're unlikely to be gentle. If I'm any judge, the longshanks will point you right. And make sure Utyrvaul goes with Ober. The myrkling's a pest, but he should keep them clear of any scouts or wayward townsfolk."

"Yes, sir," Gromic said with a bob of his head, his formality evidence of his frustration at not getting an answer. Without further comment, the big dwarf turned on his heel and went about his duty.

"Stones preserve me." The commander sighed, went into Waelon's room, and froze. "Erduna's dugs, what are you doing?"

The red-haired dwarf, still bound up in Haeda's straining girdle, attempted to rise from where he'd been heaving and grunting against a bookcase on the far wall. Unfortunately, the sharp movement proved too much for his abused ribs, and he gave a sharp hiss and pitched up against the timber construction, wheezing.

"S-sorry, s... Ugh, Pit's leaky arse." He gasped. "Sorry, sir."

Torbjorn hurried to his side and gently but firmly led him to the large bed beside the bookcase.

"The Pit's arse for certain, and your apology for good measure," the commander growled as he gingerly lowered the dwarf onto the mattress. "What were you doing?"

Waelon's breathing had slowed to an even pace, but its shortness as he gathered himself to answer was disconcerting.

"There's something behind that damned shelf." He started to raise an arm to point, only to crumple in on himself. "Erduna's dirty nethers. I think I cracked another one."

Torbjorn alternated between looking at the former ranger and the bookshelf, torn between outrage and curiosity. After a moment of scowling, he decided he was capable enough that he could do both.

"Is this your idea of resting?" he asked, moving toward the bookcase. "Instead of staying in one place so you can heal and be useful, you go treasure hunting and hurt yourself?"

Waelon let the last of his weight settle into the gentle embrace of the well-stuffed mattress with a cautious sigh. When he was certain no fresh burst of agony was incoming, he addressed his commander's question as he stared at the ceiling. Turning his head to one side was a risk at the moment.

"Not sure about treasure, sir," Waelon began, sounding apologetic. "But I know there's something behind that hunk of wood. I just thought I should find out since we didn't need any more surprises."

Torbjorn absently nodded as he assessed the stout furnishing. He ran his hand over the fine scrollwork along the frame, which bore the older style of blocky knotwork still popular among the more conservative craftsman of their people.

There was something different about these carvings, though. The woodcarver had had a steady hand and good eye and had kept the carving consistent and smooth as fit the winding of the scrolling, but there were peculiar twists and patterns tucked between the strands and branches which formed the knotwork. It was unusual for this level of intricate detail.

The dwarf commander walked the width of the bookshelf, frowning, until he came to where Waelon had been.

"I don't suppose letting anyone else know was an option, was it?" he muttered. He shuffled to put his shoulder flush with the stone wall. It was just the barest change, but he ran his hand over the knife-thin seam between the stone and the back of the bookshelf, and he felt it.

"Didn't want to bother anyone if it was nothing," Waelon explained. "I'm a bit battered if you hadn't noticed, and I didn't know if the pain was doing funny things to my mind."

The commander decided that pointing out that his injuries meant he was unfit for exploratory efforts would have been a waste of time. Also, he'd felt the innately dwarven longing to plumb a subterranean secret. Chiding the wounded ranger would be a waste of energy.

"There does seem to be something behind this bookshelf." Torbjorn grunted as he tested the resistance of the piece. "I think there is a mechanism holding it in place. Ugh… Shouldn't be… this hard to…agh, *move!*"

"Found the drafty spot, haven't you, sir?" Waelon chuckled, sounding smug enough that Torbjorn felt like stepping over and giving his ribs a tickle. "Yeah, mechanism maybe, but for the life of me, I couldn't find one on the bloody thing."

Torbjorn wanted to point out that Waelon's failed search had resulted in exerting himself to the point of injury, which was stupid. Rather than waste words, he set about conducting his own search. His scan of the bookcase was cursory, since he expected that Waelon had done a thorough job, so to avoid frustration the commander turned his attention to the rest of the room.

The trigger for the release was likely against a wall, placed where it would be accessible but not easily disturbed.

"Torbjorn?" Waelon called, still not turning his head as he heard his superior officer shuffling slowly around the room. "Did you find something?"

"Shut up and rest," Torbjorn snapped, driving Waelon into obedient silence.

That had come out more sharply than he'd intended. He thought his eyes were seeing something his mind couldn't quite register as he looked at the right-most wall. He stepped forward to peer at the spot, but as he did, he was certain he'd lost track of what he'd detected. Muttering curses under his breath, he stepped back and waited for his eyes to slide out of focus enough that he could snare a glimpse again.

There!

It was the barest alteration in the grain of the stone, but once he knew what to look for, he saw it. Traceries not carved as much as worn into the wall created the subtle impression of a knotwork pattern that spiraled around a single stone. It was a clever clue that Torbjorn doubted anyone but a dwarf would note, sensitive as the subterranean people were to stone textures.

"I've got you now," Torbjorn crowed, advancing on the spot. He reached out to work what he was certain was the trigger to release the bookcase.

"Sir!" Waelon cried through a pain-tightened throat, up on his elbows though the effort made him sweaty and pale. "Shouldn't we let the others know before we unleash what's on the other side of that bookcase? We might interrogate the humans while we are at it."

Torbjorn, caught up in the innocent excitement of his discovery, wanted to challenge the notion that there was anything to "unleash" on the other side of the bookcase. However, they didn't know that.

"Fair point," he conceded, dejected at the momentary halt to his exploration. "But hardly a fun one."

"Being an officer is hardly ever fun," the former ranger admitted. "Probably why I didn't last long as one."

Torbjorn shook his head as he drew a chisel-tipped dagger from his belt to score the stone beside the release with an arrow.

"I thought you wound up with us because you were trying to give your brother a chance to run for it after he was locked up," Torbjorn said, raising his voice to be heard over the clink and scrape of steel on stone.

"Both were true," Waelon growled as he worked his way back into a sitting position. "I suppose if I'd seen much of a future in my commission, I might've not been so rash."

Torbjorn, who'd stepped back to assess his handiwork, paused to throw a wry grin over his shoulder at the fiery-haired dwarf.

"I don't think either of us believes that," the commander declared, making for the door. "I'm going to go be sensible. In the meantime, leave that be. If I come back and find you being rash, I'm liable to add a few more cracks to your ribs."

Waelon set himself in as comfortable a position as he could manage and forced a wan smile.

"I don't make any promises," he rasped. "But I'm not sure I could even make it over there right now."

CHAPTER TWELVE

"I still don't understand what this is about, but if my son gets hurt, I swear by every god known to mortal or beast that I'll see you all pay for this."

The interrogation of the humans had gone as well as could be expected. Both confessed ignorance, even after it was established the room where the bookcase was located was Madame Reeve's quarters. In a less fraught situation, Torbjorn might have been tempted to believe them—they were just humans—but given their conflicting interests, he decided that it was best to give them an incentive to be honest.

So, after moving Waelon, Torbjorn had arranged things accordingly.

Mabon Reeve knelt before the bookshelf while Torbjorn stood by the stone he believed to be the mechanism's release. Because of where it was placed, he'd had to drag over a chair. With his hand hovering over the stone, he was eye to eye with Mabon's mother.

"I'm about to trigger the release, so I hope for your son's sake that there are no surprises on the other side."

Crysten Reeve made a sound in the back of her throat, part snort and part snarl.

"I hope so too, but I don't know because I didn't know there was anything there besides a bookshelf."

"You never felt a need to rearrange the furniture?" Haeda frowned from where she stood with a crossbow trained on Mabon.

"It's heavy, and I'm only in this room to dress or sleep," Madame Reeve declared with a vigorous shake of her head. "Why would I bother?"

"I'd eventually want to rearrange," Haeda muttered. "Though I've never had a—"

"Not to be rude," Mabon interrupted, making a valiant effort not to look terrified, "but can we just go ahead and find out if I am about to die? I am tired of the terror, and I'd just like to get on with this."

Torbjorn gave an appreciative chuff, only to find the lad's mother glaring at him like she would induce his beard to burst into flame with hateful looks alone. As the dwarf commander touched the stone, he wasn't certain the seething woman couldn't accomplish that, given enough time and incentive.

For an awful instant, Torbjorn felt that nothing would give way, and his stomach twisted in a spasm of embarrassed disappointment. They'd allowed fatigue and fear to work them into a tizzy, and here he was, pressing his hand to the wall as though trying to hold it up. He'd have to face that there was nothing behind the bookshelf, or the mechanism to move the stout furnishing could only be located in an even more esoteric manner. He wasn't sure which would be worse.

As he leaned his weight into his hand, the stone shifted. One side sank while the other rose, and there was a heavy *ka-click* behind the rocky panel. Then the faintest sound of heavy gears rumbling round somewhere behind the stones, and the bookshelf gave a creaking whine as it slid to one side.

At nearly the same instant, Crysten Reeve cried out. "Mabon, drop!" she shrieked, rushing toward him with her arms outstretched as though to flatten him. "Drop flat."

Several things happened.

The young man obeyed his mother's command, which spared him another dwarvish bolt with his name on it. The bolt buzzed over his sinking head like an angry hornet and passed through the yawning black portal opening behind the bookshelf. Torbjorn didn't see where the bolt had gone because he was preoccupied with snaring Mabon's mother.

One hand grabbed the woman's sleeve and achieved a twisting grip while his other hand grasped his magsax. Either because of the unsteadiness of the chair's construction, given its human craftsmanship, or sheer surprise at the force of the human's efforts, the dwarf commander tumbled off his perch. Dwarf and woman descended to the unforgiving stone floor, bound together by a fiercely gripped sleeve.

"*GROMIC!*" Haeda bellowed as she furiously worked the lever of her crossbow while stomping toward the supine Mabon.

"Get off me," Madame Reeve screamed, twisting and flailing. "We have to shut it! Shut it now!"

Torbjorn's head had bounced off the floor when he'd landed with no hand free to catch him since he struggled with a woman in one hand and his sword in the other. For a moment, the commander's senses swam, his vision watery at the edges. With a spluttering shake of his head, he saw that he'd managed to keep hold of both things in his hands. He snarled and yanked Crysten to one side, then flung himself over her. The spirited matron was stronger than he would have given her credit for, but it took only a little more effort to twist her wriggling arm behind her back and place his knee on her spine.

With a flick of his wrist, he pressed the magsax's blade against her bobbing throat.

"Hold still!" he growled in her ear. "Any more, and I open your throat."

Straining to look up, the woman managed to meet his gaze. Her face was terrified.

"Please!" She gulped, the effort causing the sharp blade to open a thin line across her throat. "You have to close the passage."

Mabon saw the thin tracery of red on his mother's throat and a roar sprang from his chest.

"LET HER GO!" he bellowed. He got to one knee, ready to spring. *"GET OFF MY MO—"*

The command was cut short as the thick stock of Haeda's duabuw crashed into the young man's head. Driven by rage, the incensed son ignored the fresh gash on the other side of his skull and managed to twist around to face Haeda. Before he could leap forward with fingers curled into vengeful claws, the dwarfess struck the snarling face before her.

Mabon's head snapped back, and he fell back with a thump before tumbling over to lie on one side, eyes unfocused.

Gromic burst into the room just then, his duabuw in one hand, magsax in the other, blue eyes blazing.

"Gromic, cover the tunnel," Torbjorn barked. He rose to his feet, awkwardly hauling Madame Reeve up with him. The woman arced back to keep the commander's blade from opening her neck from jaw to collarbone, her pleading unabated.

"Please hurry," she pressed, trying to keep her voice steady despite her painful position. "Seal it before it is too late."

"Shut up," Torbjorn snapped, shuffling toward the wall with the release. "Haeda, secure Master Reeve before he gets hurt worse."

The driver replied, "Yes, sir," as she stepped toward the human. With her crossbow still in hand, she was nearly on top of him. In short order, Mabon, mouth still slack and eyes refusing to settle on anything, was hogtied on the floor.

"We're running out of time!" Crysten cried, her composure

cracking as her eyes darted from the wall-mounted release to the black tunnel and back. "Shut it while we still can!"

"Gromic," Torbjorn bellowed, refusing to give up his grip on the human or his sword. "What do you see?"

The stout dwarf had reversed his grip on his sword to brace his duabuw between pommel and hand with the stock resting on his shoulder. The point of the loaded bolt tracked with his searching eyes.

"Nothing but worked stone, sir," Gromic answered. "But there's some...something moving at the far end of the tunnel. Can't see it so much as feel it and...and smell it."

Crysten Reeve began to issue another plea and Torbjorn twisted her arm hard, driving the woman to her knees. He let the tip of his sword prick her under the chin, drawing a cry of pain.

"What's going on?" he demanded, his dark eyes boring into hers. "No more lies!"

"I'll tell you," she panted, every trace of her proud, commanding presence washed away as she looked at the darkened passage. "Just please, let me seal it."

At that instant, the temperature in the room plummeted, an icy gust issuing from the mouth of the tunnel.

"Torbjorn," Gromic called, his voice rising in pitch.

The dwarf commander shot a glance at the dwarf standing before the night-filled cavity, his breath streaming out in an icy cloud. The stone framing the tunnel began to blossom with jagged tendrils of frost, and the darkness within seemed to congeal.

"Do it," he commanded as he released the woman's arm and withdrew his sword. "Quickly."

Needing no further urging, Crysten Reeve sprang up and hammered the upraised edge of stone with her palm. There was another *ka-click* within the wall, but the bookshelf did not slide in the opposite direction. It launched itself back into place with a whir of gears and the slither of chains within the walls. The speed of its return was enough to toss books and curios from the shelves across the floor. Even with so quick a return, Torbjorn still caught the briefest impression of something pale and withered straining to catch the edge of the shelf. Torbjorn's heart twisted in his chest as the passage sealed once more with a creaking thump.

Behind the bookshelf, something sharp raked across the wood, then there was a pained hiss. Then they all felt a sudden absence in the passage beyond, along with the rising temperature in the room.

For a moment none dared speak, each consumed by their churning thoughts.

"What was that th—"

Torbjorn's question was cut short as a thin, twisting laugh reached their ears, sending a fresh spur of ice down every spine. When another voice rose in the stillness, every soul, dwarf and human, jumped.

"Commander!" Tomza shouted, pounding on the wall of her room. "Torbjorn, what's going on?"

CHAPTER THIRTEEN

"I'm beginning to wonder if one of us did something to offend the Shaper. I mean, personally."

"Ober, don't say that." Tomza grunted as she adjusted her position on the stool. "He might hear you and wonder if He missed something. Could you fetch my bag?"

The young dwarf frowned across the barn, an expression that had not left his face since his sister shared what had occurred in his absence. He stumped over to the satchel, which was out of his sister's reach near the horse stalls. They'd been sent to the outbuilding shortly after Ober had returned. Torbjorn was eager for Tomza to begin her work, but not for the humans to have any inkling of what was about to occur.

His approach made the two horses shuffle in their stalls and give nervous snorts. A petulant urge to shout and pull a wild face at the beasts arose, but Ober squashed it when he saw their fearful glances. Horses were not typical beasts of burden among his kind, that honor going to various porcine creatures. Staring at the powerful creatures penned up over matters not their own, he couldn't help feeling a kinship with their plight.

They were all prisoners entrapped in schemes of others, and no matter their strength, they had little control. They could thrash about, but what would that do but hurt themselves and those they loved?

Ober shook his head to dismiss the worrisome thoughts and tore his eyes from the creatures in the stalls.

"I'm serious," the young dwarf insisted, handing the satchel to his sister. "From what you found in Momma's books to the grove to everything that put us here, it feels like everything is against us."

Without preamble, Tomza plunged into the satchel, fetching out more ingredients to go with what her brother had brought her. She tried not to think about how the lichen she used to steep the mona root was running low, but her eyes kept wandering to the sparse shavings in the bottom of the bottle. As the cold set in, the lichen would be hard to find. They'd have to hew into the trees to get what she needed, making its collection more tedious and obvious. This would be less of a concern once they reached the Pickets, but it was a long way to the southern edge of the dwarven territory.

"*Everything* can't be against us," she murmured, staring into the nearly empty satchel. "We're still alive, aren't we?"

Ober was too deep in his own ruminations to know that she was talking to herself rather than him, but the words provoked a burst of laughter like a sour cough.

"There are worse things than death," he growled, his gray eyes distant and troubled. "I never understood. I now know it would have been better if—"

The leather satchel hurtled through the air to hit Ober's face with a dull thud.

"What the—" he spluttered, one half-raised hand catching the strap of the bag as he snapped a sharp look at his sister. She was snarling at him.

"Shut up!" she raged as her finger rose to stab accusingly toward his chest. "I don't want to hear that kak come out of your mouth ever again, you hear me? Not ever again."

Ober gaped for a heartbeat, confusion and anger wrestling in his mind as his mouth issued a series of half-formed sounds. When he finally spoke, anger won the contest, though it was a far colder fury than his sister's bombastic display.

"Tomza, you don't understand. You *can't* understand," he insisted, his hands curling into trembling fists. "You don't know what it's like to have this…this thing inside of you. This monster under your skin that wants to get out, and you're scared that deep inside, you want it to get out. You don't know what it's like to wrestle that kind of temptation every day and feel that you can't even trust yourself to keep others safe."

Tomza's laugh was like the peel of shattering bells.

"Really? You don't think I understand temptation?" she hissed, her face twisting into an acidic smile. "Do you think all I learned from Momma's books was how to heal and mend? Do you think all those pages were filled with curatives and techniques to ensure a healthy baby? Or are you going to pretend that you didn't feel what crawled through the pages of Momma's *Night Book* the day we heard the wight's forces were coming?"

Ober didn't speak, and he couldn't meet her gaze as a shiver prickled up his spine.

"Knowledge is power. Momma and Poppa both taught us that," she continued. "And every day, every single day, since we lost our home, I've had to fight the urge to use my knowledge to get revenge, so don't you dare talk to me about temptation as a justification for giving up. I've carried that weight longer than you, and if I'm not quitting, you can bet your arse you don't get to either!"

Ober's eyes flashed, and his mouth opened to offer a scathing retort, but he paused, thinking better of it. The icy strength of his anger left him, and his shoulders sank as his head swayed from side to side.

"Maybe...maybe you're stronger than I am." He shrugged, eyes heavy with tears. "And in the end, it still isn't the same since I know it will happen someday. I won't have any mona root prepared, or it will be a weak batch, and this thing inside of me will tear out of me. I'll kill you and anyone and everyone else near me."

Tomza forced her eyes to stay fixed on her brother as she spoke and not dart toward the nearly expended store of lichen.

"You didn't kill me when the savagelings attacked us," she stated, recalling that awful day. "I ran over to you when I saw the change taking you, hoping I could help, I think, but you changed and attacked the others, not me."

"I slaughtered everyone!" Ober cried, his burning grief giving him the strength to meet her eyes. "Every dwarf we'd trained with, marched with, fought with... Every dwan we pledged to stand beside and who'd pledged to stand beside us. I tore them all to pieces as that thing laughed inside me!"

"But not me," Tomza repeated, her face set as though she could subdue her brother's tormented spirit through sheer will. "The beast spirit used you to kill the others, even the dwan we served with, but when it was at its strongest, it couldn't force you to kill me."

Ober ground a palm against one eye, then the other as he was held captive in his sister's stare.

"I suppose so." He sniffed, his voice thin as he fought to keep from sobbing. "But what does that mean, that I wanted to kill the others but not you? The monster only kills those I want to die, like my brothers in arms?"

Tomza shook her head even as her shoulders rose in a stiff shrug.

"I don't exactly know, Ober. I really don't," she muttered,

holding her brother's tearful gaze. "But I think you still have some control. That gives me hope that not all is lost, and I'm going to hold onto that hope with both hands. Can't you hold on with me?"

Ober took several breaths, and then, after once more swiping at his eyes, he managed a heavy nod.

"I-I'll try." He swallowed heavily, and his throat gave a soft click.

"That's all any of us can do." Tomza sighed, deflated and listless on the stool. "Now, let's see if we can't get me up on my own two feet so you don't have to keep carrying me everywhere."

Ober nodded and took a step back. He knew this would make little or no difference to the working, but it felt appropriate. Tomza had long become inured to the embarrassment of her brother looking away as though her magic were shameful. He could not watch her do the things that had been passed from mother to daughter in their family for generations.

Her mother had prepared her for this reality, but being out here among the horses by Torbjorn's orders rankled more than she'd expected. She understood the practical considerations, but she'd seen the relief in Haeda's and Gromic's eyes when she'd left. She also knew that when they hauled Waelon out to be healed, she'd see his anxious trepidation before he looked away in shame.

"Focus," she murmured, gathering a handful of spindly mushrooms and some slivers of willow bark. "No distractions."

Using the breathing techniques she'd been taught, Tomza narrowed her mind to a single point of focus and allowed quavering sounds to rise from her throat. The tiny sparks of power within the ingredients of her working flickered within her hand, and for a moment, she felt the warmth of cinders between her fingers without the pain that should have come from them. Thin plumes of smoke wafted from between her fingers as she bent over her wounded leg, and the earth-scented smoke curled and fluttered around her shin and slid down and around her ankle, ephemeral snakes probing at the swollen joint.

This working was different than when she healed others. It was odd to feel the current of power weaving through her and looping back on itself. She felt a thrumming potency, not quite pain and not quite pleasure, with the potential for either. All it would take was for her to surrender to its embrace and let that reservoir, tapped by ancient syllables, flow free until it flooded out of her in a torrent of anguished ecstasy, a birth unshackled by crude matter.

Tomza's voice buzzed with the working as the inflammation was washed from her ankle, the joint's painful stiffness suddenly absent as the flesh shrank and the tracks where the strips of cloth had held fast smoothed. The cinders left her fingers, ingredients reduced to ashes, the serpentine strands of smoke still coiled her leg. It would have been so easy to let them do their work, washing over her, soothing every ache, restoring every weary bit of her…

So easy, but where would it end?

No, she'd learned at her mother's knee and in the fires of their home. She'd learned at her mother's death.

"Enough," she breathed, and with a wave of her ash-covered hand, she scattered the remaining energies and waited for the wave of fatigue to come. This time, it was like the creeping ache of a fever. She knew her ankle was mended and she could rise and walk about, but her body seemed intent on convincing her otherwise.

"Did it work?" Ober asked, stepping forward after looking to see if the unnatural phenomenon was gone. "I didn't get the wrong ingredients, did I?"

"No, you did fine," Tomza announced with a deep sigh. "But I'm not sure I'll be up to mending Waelon just yet. I'll need rest and food."

Ober nodded and held out a hand. She waved him off, then braced herself with hands on knees and drove upward.

"Steady," the young dwarf warned, holding out his arms to catch his sister as she tested her repaired ankle. "No need to rush."

Tomza gave Ober an incredulous scowl as she bent and tugged the scraps of cloth off her ankle.

"Ober," she began, using the know-it-all tone any big sister worthy of the name masters before her sibling can walk, "we're being chased by a wight lord's army, there are still probably savagelings skulking about, and there's Pit knows what hiding in the basement of the house we are hiding in. If there was ever a time to rush things, it is now."

He frowned but didn't argue the point, just stepped around his sister and began tucking things into her satchel.

"No, let me get that," she said. "I've got a system, and no matter how many times I tell you, you always muck it up."

Ober gave a small laugh, knowing his sister's system was mostly her shoving things into random pockets and remembering where she put them. He moved to the barn door to peek outside. The homestead was secluded and the weather bitter enough that visitors were unlikely. It still wouldn't do to have some particularly bold guest come traipsing over the frosted ground to see a dwan strolling about like he owned the place.

For his caution and thoughtfulness, Ober was rewarded with the sight of eight figures stomping down the trail toward the house. He quickly adjusted his stance to hide behind the door as he gave a soft cluck of his tongue. Tomza's head snapped up to see her brother flattening himself against the barn door while he unslung his duabuw.

The dwarfess choked back a curse, scooped up her duabuw, and moved to the other side of the barn door. Her limbs felt like lead and it was an effort to keep her lids from drooping, but her ankle proved capable of bearing her weight without complaint.

"Those longshanks bastards betrayed us?" she hissed to Ober as she primed the crossbow and tried to steal a glance into the yard. "They got word out for help?"

"Don't see how," Ober muttered, shaking his head as he watched the bulky figures approach. "We've kept them all tied up except for nature breaks, and even then, they've never left the rooms except the two who were there when they opened the tunnel."

Burly bodies swaddled in heavy coats and hides, the intruders seemed more brutish than their ugly faces conveyed. Their features looked mean, yet they evidenced crude humor and mischief as winks and chuckles passed between them. Being Valeborn, Ober had experience with reading human ages. Several of them were what passed for middle age among humans, but their demeanor was that of young toughs up to no good.

Given that he saw heavy hewing implements, cleavers and hatchets in place of swords and battle axes, Ober knew their visit did not bode well for anyone.

"Maybe that thing in the tunnel fetched them," Tomza whispered as she set the stock of her duabuw to her shoulder. "It only makes sense that the tunnel lets out somewhere, and for all we know, it ran off to fetch help."

Ober silenced his sister with a wave of his hand. The men were getting closer, but they didn't look at the barn. Their attention was fixed on the house. Ober thought he might be able to hear them, which meant they might hear her.

"Quiet," Ober mouthed, raising his crossbow to take aim at the hindmost man. His ears strained to shut out the snuffling of the horses and his pounding heart.

"I'm saying it now," one of the rough men said. "The girl's mine first. I'm not sliding me plow into anything what's already been furrowed."

Others raised their voices in protest, having their hearts set on a similar objective. All of them fell quiet when the tallest of their number gave a soft laugh. The silken sound was at odds with man's pox-cratered face and meaty hands, which played with the bone-handle of a hunting knife longer than Ober's forearm.

"Oh, come off it, Yal," the man teased, his thin lips curdling into a mocking smile. "We all know you only take the fresh ones because if anyone else's been in the field, your little plow'll slide right through without touching soil."

The churlish guffaws which rose at the jest had Ober wincing in disgust. Yal's face purpled, and his tongue lashed across his lips several times before he could master himself enough to string a few snarled words together.

"Lying bastard!" he spat, his hands at his wide belt but noticeably clear of the hatchet and knife that hung there. "I'll drop trow and show you my plow right here, Owyn."

That sparked more raw chuckles from the men as Owyn, who was clearly the leader of the group, stepped toward the door of the house.

"Time enough for that," the tall man declared with a suggestive nod at the door. He lowered his voice to a whisper Ober could barely make out. "Though no need to give the game away right from the jump. After all, Crysten still thinks she can barter her way out of this."

"Stupid quim," another man snarled to the grunting nods of his fellows.

"Oi, think she'll offer you a roll in the big bed like last time? You know, to spare her girl?" pondered a thug standing beside Yal. "Might be fun to have her willing before we take what we want."

"Maybe," the leader drawled, his eyes wandering around the yard as though looking for something. "Though if Dillon's about, I might get too excited by thinking of taking his gray nag in front of him to manage anything so refined."

"Oh, Owyn'd out-mean an Ol' Whitey!" several of the gang

declared joyously amid more barks of laughter before their leader quieted them with a finger to his lips.

"Quiet now," the tall man chided with another foul smile as he raised his hand to knock on the door. "Time to talk to the lady of the house, so mind your manners."

CHAPTER FOURTEEN

"This is quite the predicament."

"Thank you for the keen observation, elf," Torbjorn growled as he motioned Madame Reeve over to him. "Please keep us posted on further developments."

The svartalf cut a flourishing salute with one long hand as he threw a wink at the dwarf and then at the woman shuffling stiffly forward.

"Duly noted, sir," he replied.

The dwarf commander flapped a hand for Utyrvaul to take up a position opposite Gromic on the other side of the door. At the rear of the room, Haeda was atop the table, duabuw leveled at the door. Torbjorn noted that Crysten's sharp gaze took all this in. She staggered toward her captor on legs grown unsteady with close confinement. As she met the commander's eyes, he also noted the eager spark of vengeful, defiant hope that she didn't bother to hide as she glared at him.

"It seems we may be expecting company," she observed archly. "I'm assuming you'd like me to get the door?"

Torbjorn bit back the angry threats he wanted to send back

into the woman's superior expression. He knew doing so would make him look weak. In his experience, a leader accomplished more with a level head and a facade of calm. That and he didn't want to give the longshanks the benefit of seeing him sweat.

"First," he said, every word pitched to exude calm authority, "I'd like you to take a peek through the shutter to see if you recognize anyone, though I'd advise you to make it quick and make no noise, please."

"As you wish," the woman said with a toss of her head, sending her disheveled hair to one side as she stepped to the window. Outside, several men enjoyed a rude joke a half-dozen steps from the front door.

Torbjorn tried not to tense as he watched Crysten lean against the window, but his fingers tightened around the hilt of his magsax as she peered between the slats. Was this going to be where she would do something foolish that neither of them could turn back from? The dwarf commander steeled himself for what might come next, even as he recoiled with disgust and dread.

This was not why he'd become a soldier.

"Watchman's shining arse," Matron Reeve swore as she lurched back from the window. Her face had lost all color, and she was at a loss for words. The crunch of heavy steps on the frosted earth sounded amid more coarse chatter just beyond the door.

"Who are they?" Torbjorn hissed, his eyes darting between the door and the woman.

"Thugs, brutes… Bad men," Crysten replied. "We owe them money, and they've come to collect…again."

Torbjorn didn't need to ask if the Reeves had the funds on hand—not just because their search of the home had produced very little currency, but because of the flush of color that came into the woman's frightened face as she spoke of her family's debts. Not for the first or last time did Torbjorn's pity go out to the widow. A hard hand had settled over her life, and it seemed unlikely to change anytime soon.

"Get as many of them inside as you can," Torbjorn said, turning to the others in the room. "Tuck in and let 'em get closer."

Crysten Reeve didn't seem keen on this as Haeda ducked under the table and Gromic and Utyrvaul sidled away from the door to lurk behind the furnishings. The woman's attention was ripped back toward the door when a sharp knock sounded. One hand reached toward the handle as she shot a last glance at the dwarf commander, but he'd shuffled out of sight, denying her final hope as her hand settled on the latch.

"One moment," she managed to croak as she fought to steady herself, fingers numb even as they trembled.

"Don't bother getting decent on my account," came a wicked purr that could only have been Owyn. "I'd actually prefer it otherwise."

Outside, the cackles and hoots of the tall man's sycophants rose in chorus, but rather than hardening the grip of the ice in Crysten's heart, the cacophony fired the faltering flame of her indignation. She'd been forced to endure hairy-fisted dwarfs nosing around her home, and then she'd had to watch as the…the thing in the tunnels nearly took her son. All this and more had been foisted on her, but she still had the choice to refuse to let Owyn and his cronies see her afraid. She might die in the chaos that followed, but she'd be damned if she would give the towering stack of filth the pleasure of seeing her shake before him.

The latch rose, and Madame Reeve glared into the cold eyes of the debt collector.

"What are you doing here?" she demanded, but she didn't pause to hear an answer. "I've still got two weeks, according to the last meeting I had with Gwilym."

The ringleader was taken aback by the speed and force of the matron's delivery. He recovered after a brief pause, his face resuming its leering smile.

"Seems things have changed, and not in your favor, I'm afraid," he began, edging half a step over the threshold. "The boss heard tell the other night that a militia patrol was found dead. The whole lot of them was snuffed out by a band of badger rangers being chased by the ol' wheezy that came over the mountain a few days ago."

Madame Reeve forced her gaze to remain fixed on Owyn as she gave ground. From the corner of her eye, she thought she saw the others creeping forward like vermin heading toward a dying creature, cautious but eager.

"You know we don't get much in the way of news out here," she retorted with a dismissive shrug, surrendering another half a step. "But I don't see what the bailiff's missing men have to do with Gwilym's and my arrangement."

"Don't you?" Owyn crooned, now in the house. His posse shuffled toward the door. "From what he understands, your boy —Mabon, is it?—well, he was leading that little party that bought it. The bodies haven't been brought back for identification yet, but your boy is either dead from badger steel, or he's been captured. We all know that means he's as good as dead with those stunted bastards."

Crysten panicked as the others pressed into the room. She was certain they would spot the stout dwarf lurking behind the chest of drawers or the elf peeking from the coat rack, but eight pairs of bloodshot eyes were on her. The last of the men came through the door, practically pressing her against the hearth.

"The debt wasn't my son's," Crysten rasped. Her throat felt dry and tight. "So again, I don't see why you're here?"

"Ol' Whitey's danglers, that's cold," Owyn crowed as he wagged his head. "All business, even with her baby boy a frostbitten corpse in some crag. I wonder if that ice in your heart's spread south?"

As though to demonstrate his lurid curiosity, the tall man's hand snaked out and tugged the woman's skirt. Mistress Reeve swatted the hand away as the men crowed and whistled, but that only made them mock her louder.

"Mabon being dead or alive doesn't change the agreement I made with your boss," Crysten declared. "So, you've got no business here."

Owyn's hand curled into a fist, and his smile widened on his gaunt, scarred face.

"Gwilym sees it differently," the tall man said. "Without the boy and his pay from the bailiff, there's no way you can pay him back or even scrape together enough for another payment to buy more time."

"That's my business," Mistress Reeve shot back, looking behind her to keep from stumbling into the hearth.

"Gwilym saw fit to make it my business."

She looked up to see something hard and bestial in Owyn's eyes, no laugh touching his twisted smile.

"Come here," he snarled, the words violent as he lunged forward.

Forewarned by the look in the man's eyes, Crysten tried to twist away from the grasping hand. Pinned as she was against the hearth, she only evaded the first grab before long, hard fingers snared her hair. She screamed and fought to pry his fingers away, but a knobby fist slammed into her stomach, knocking the wind out of her.

"Just take it, and it'll be over quicker than you think," Owyn said as he dragged Crysten to her toes, nearly nose to nose with the gasping woman.

"Funny," came a gruff, guttural voice. "I was just about to tell you the same."

Two duabuws spoke their bellicose language as heavy bolts punched through flesh. One buried itself in the skull of a brute with a squashed nose, the end of its fletched shaft jutting out like a comically festooned prosthetic for the eradicated snout. The other tore through the belly of a man before driving into another, punching a neat hole through the front of his breeches. Both men screamed, one pitched notably higher than the other.

"Badgers!" one thug roared, tugging a cleaver off his belt, only to be parted from his arm at the elbow by the keen edge of the Reeve family sword.

"Not as homogenous as all that," Utyrvaul corrected as he smoothly slid the sword into the disarmed man's chest. "I'm sure you don't even know what that word means, poor fellow."

The humans recoiled from the elf that loomed half a head over Owyn and found a less eloquent barrier in the growling form of Gromic on their other flank.

Half their party was downed before two stuttering heartbeats had passed, and the rest were hemmed in. Owyn's collection posse drew their weapons like cornered dogs showing their teeth. Their towering leader had kept his grip on Crysten's hair as he pinned her against him, his hunting knife raised before him. His frightened and frantic companions tried to creep back to the door.

"What is this?" he snarled in Crysten's ear, watching a sturdy dark-haired dwarf step around the central fireplace. Even a base creature like Owyn Blaen could feel the command radiating off the squat figure, and that stoked his rage and terror.

"These are the last few moments of your life," the dwarf said, his broad-bladed sword in hand at his side. "No two ways about it."

Owyn gnashed his teeth as he crept back farther. The hunting knife withdrew to press against Crysten's throat, not far from where the commander's magsax had been that morning.

"Not another step," the ringleader hissed, eyes darting about the room before settling on Torbjorn once more. "We're walking out of here, or I open the bitch's throat."

Torbjorn held the man's wild eyes, ignoring Crysten's pleading gaze.

"You're not listening, longshanks," Torbjorn replied softly. "You're a dead man. Cutting her will mean you die slower, though I'm sure you've heard about us badger rangers. We can make a man's death take a long time when we want to."

Owyn's hands trembled so badly he nicked Crysten, eliciting a hiss of pain.

"W-we can w-work something out," he stammered, creeping back as the men around him inched away. "My b-boss is a r-rich man. He'll p-pay well for us."

"Oh, I plan on visiting Gwilym," Torbjorn assured the tall man. "But that's not your problem anymore."

"Badger scum!" shrieked one of the terrified thugs as he rushed forward with a farrier's hammer in one hand and a hatchet in the other.

Torbjorn didn't bother to duck as Haeda's crossbow gave a rejoinder that had the man crumpling, weapons abandoned to paw at the bolt in his throat.

"S-steady now," Owyn growled, though whether he was talking to his enemies or his two remaining compatriots wasn't clear. "There's no rea—"

"Sod Gwilym," squealed the man behind Owyn as he spun toward the door. He managed to tear it open just before Utyrvaul hewed him from crown to teeth. The dying fellow toppled to one side, nearly dragging the sword out of the svartalf's grip. The last of Owyn's thugs seized his opportunity and sprang through the open door before anyone could stop him.

Torbjorn watched the man's flight through the open door, only to see the man stagger after a sound from the barn.

Owyn looked around the room and saw nothing but death, from the corpses of his men to the hard eyes of the dwarfs and the elf. Every last pretense was stripped away as something hot and wet ran down his leg. He threw down his knife and shoved the woman away. With hands upraised, he sank down to kneel in his own piss, voice raised in a piteous wail.

"Mercy! Please!" he screeched, eyes bulging as tears and snot ran freely. "I was just doing what the boss told me! I was—"

Before anyone else could respond, Crysten Reeve bent to snatch up the discarded knife. She swiveled, still crouched, and drove the blade into the man's soiled groin. Owyn gave a shrill squeal as his knife bit deep, then she sawed upward as though intent on cutting the man in half.

Blind instinct drove Owyn to shove the woman away from him. She took the knife with her, trailing a red mess from the torn space between his legs. His faltering instincts also drove him to feebly clutch his ravaged nethers, which meant he could only watch as the crimson point of his knife rammed through his eye. The last thing Owyn Blaen heard was Crysten Reeve's frenzied scream as his knife was driven home.

Torbjorn watched it all, his mouth a grim line under his mustache. The bloodstained woman tore the knife free and, her scream becoming sobs, stabbed the shuddering corpse over and over. The dwarf commander frowned, then nodded to Gromic.

The stout dwarf sheathed his sword and slung his shield over his shoulder before stepping forward.

"All right, easy now, lass," he cooed gently, taking the upraised knife in a firm grip. "It's over."

Crysten, her body shaking with sobs, released her hold on the knife to beat her fists on the dead man's face and chest. The former fordwan cast the bloodied blade aside to wrap an arm around the woman and drag her away.

"It's over now," Gromic repeated, steadily drawing her away as Ober and Tomza appeared in the doorway.

"We got the runner," Ober offered. Torbjorn nodded, noting that Tomza was standing on her own two feet.

"Are you ready to tend to Waelon?" he asked, his magsax returning to its scabbard without a thought.

Tomza managed a tenuous nod.

"I could get ready," she offered.

"Then do it," Torbjorn instructed coolly, looking at the seven bodies. "We're officially running out of time."

CHAPTER FIFTEEN

Mabon had never been so scared in all his life.

Not when he'd looked down the length of a blade at the svartalf.

Not during the shuffling walk down the mountain with a rope about his neck.

Not when he'd seen…well, not even during the moment with the tunnel.

No, it was the eternal moments he spent lying in the dark, struggling uselessly against his bonds as he heard the sharp sounds of violence and the screaming sobs of his mother. Dillon swore and snarled like a caged animal, and Kai whimpered pitifully. Mabon writhed in his bonds until he collapsed, breathless and sweating, against his brother.

"What's happening, Mabon?" Hadyn cried, his voice lighter and higher than Mabon remembered.

The young man was glad his little brother couldn't see his tears. His body was cramping with spasms that were part exertion, part terror. Another savage burst of energy saw him wrestling with his bonds again. He pondered what he would even do if he managed to conquer the coils trapping him here. That voice in his head, more honest than most, told him it understood it was better to squirm and struggle than lie impotent and listen to his mother's cries.

"Mabon?" Hadyn asked. "What is happening?"

Mabon collapsed again, everything hurting. Before this, he'd never appreciated all the shades of darkness, but now they all swam together until he was certain he would be sick. His head still ached abominably from the bludgeoning by the older female dwarf. His neck felt as though the muscles had been replaced by rigid rods intent on painfully holding his head immobile. In his momentary grappling with his bonds, he'd managed to make everything hurt worse and achieved nothing.

Iridescent patches bloomed across his field of vision. He lay there wheezing, unsure if blood or sweat slicked his wrists and ankles. Given how they burned, it was blood. He was distracted from his miserable contemplations when he noticed a silence had fallen over the house. In it, Mabon achieved an even greater depth of fear. It reached a perfect pitch that had his heart shriveling in his chest as he lay there, hearing nothing.

"It's stopped." Mabon's little brother sobbed, his wretched cries painfully loud in ominous silence. "Why has it stopped, Mabon?"

The young man lay shaking and gasping on the floor, heart hammering in his chest. He was certain he was about to die. He should have said something to his brother, offered some deceitful reassurance or some searing truth. Anything other than lying there, hunched and useless. With their father dead, he was the man of the house, wasn't he? It was his job to be strong and brave and protect everyone, wasn't it?

Then why, Watchman damn him, did he just keep lying there?

"Mabon?" Hadyn murmured, but a sharp hiss from Dillon silenced him.

"Quiet, boy," the tough old servant instructed, his decorum

forgotten as he strained to listen for sound above them. "I think I hear something."

Up above, there were dull thumps, and something was slid across the floor.

Mabon felt Kai shift to cling to his father. He couldn't see it, but he felt the change. In his mind, he formed the picture of the manservant's craggy face pointed upward, his expression grim, as his son clung to him as best he could while bound. That vision, so clear in his mind's eye despite the cornucopia of nothing before his eyes, stirred more in Mabon than pain, fear, and shame.

It drove strength and will into his body, and with a grunt, he lurched upright, managing to lean his shoulder against his brother's.

"I don't know," he whispered, his voice not partaking of the strength flowing through his body. "But we're going to have to face the results, so all we can do is…is be brave."

Shame gripped him, but as quickly as it had pounced, he shook it off. What use was shame if these were his last moments? He'd failed his mother, but would he do even worse by failing his brother and Dillon and his son? Shame wouldn't change what had come before and would not improve what came next. That truth was clear.

Overhead there were the sounds of heavy boots and gruff voices. Mabon told himself that meant the dwarfs had won whatever scuffle had occurred, but with his newfound clarity, that meant nothing. The only thing that mattered was holding fast and true as long as he could.

"Mabon?" Hadyn hissed in his ear.

"Yes?" he answered softly. "What is it?"

He could feel his little brother gathering himself to speak.

"Is Momma dead?"

The question came in the voice of a child years Hadyn's junior, quivering and sincere.

"I don't—" Mabon began, then heavy steps came down the stairs and boots scuffed on the stone passage outside their door.

"Just be brave, Hadyn," he intoned, the words coming out quickly since they had little time before the door opened. Deep-set eyes caught the gleam of the light in the hall as they swept over the prisoners to settle on Mabon. For the first time, the young man was unafraid.

"Be brave," he repeated as the dwarf stomped forward and began to drag him through the door. "Hadyn, be brave."

"What's happened up there?" Dillon growled. "Damn you, where's Crysten?"

The dwarf refused to speak until the rope that bound Mabon to the others went taut and Hadyn and Kai were pulled across the floor.

"Bones' knobby prick," Gromic cursed irritably. "I knew this would be a pain in the arse."

Mabon was roughly rolled over, and hard fingers tugged at the ropes. Mabon used the moment to look at his brother, his pale face catching the light from the open door.

"Be brave, Hadyn," he said, the words a chant like those the Priest-Sentinel repeated at the altar. "Be brave."

"Where's Mistress Reeve?" Dillon demanded, his hoarse voice cracking as it rose to a shout. "What've you done to her? Filthy badger, answer me!"

Kai began to sob openly, the wrenching sounds muffled by his father's shoulder.

"Kak on this," the stout dwarf hissed, then there was the steely whisper of a blade leaving its sheath. Something cold and sharp passed his still-bound hands, and the sharp point pricked his cramping back.

"You bastards! You stunted, murderous bastards!" Dillon screamed. Kai's sobs were a keening wail.

"Be brave, Hadyn," Mabon repeated, forcing himself to speak steadily and hold his brother's eyes. "Be brave."

Mabon wondered what it would be like to die, the thought devoid of the horror it had once held. He had moments long enough to consider it since time seemed to crawl by. If this was an end, it seemed to be in no rush.

Then the cruel grip of the ropes left his limbs, and he was dragged up.

"Go on, lad," the dwarf said, setting Mabon on unsteady feet. "Up the stairs with you."

Mabon blinked, then staggered along, guided by the hand that was clamped around one arm. He was through the door before he realized it, then he was twisting around to try to meet Hadyn's eyes again. His certainty, once so solid he could have stood upon it, crumbled.

Gromic closed the door before the brothers' eyes met. Then the young man was half led, half dragged toward the stairs, and icy sweat broke out on his body again.

"Momma!"

Torbjorn hid his wince at the human's cry as he came into the room and saw his bloodstained mother seated at the table.

The young man lurched forward but was kept from reaching the woman by Gromic's grip on his arm. Mabon strained forward until the dwarf commander gave a nod, then the boy was released.

"I'm…" Crysten Reeve began, but her words caught in her throat, and it took her a moment to gather herself. "I'm all right, Mabon. It's not my blood. I-I…"

Her voice devolved into soft sobs as her son wrapped his arms around her. She pressed her face into his chest, and they clung to each other, mother buried in the shelter of her son's firm embrace. The young man stared around the room, his eyes bouncing from one splash of blood to the next. His gaze settled on the thick pool just in front of the door. On the lower level, the shouts and cries of the other humans could be heard. They were faint and fading things before the muffled weeping of the woman and the slow, heavy breaths of the boy.

The moment stretched until Haeda emerged from downstairs, the girl in tow. "Torbjorn," she called, hands over the child's ears. "They are raising a fuss. I think they're under the impression that we're killing those two."

The driver shot a meaningful look at the girl, then noticed the little one's eyes were fixed on the blood-smeared Mistress Reeve. Haeda gave an exasperated splutter as she moved to block the child's line of sight, still looking pointedly toward her commander.

Torbjorn sighed and glanced at Gromic.

"Please go downstairs and explain that none of their people was hurt," the dwarf leader instructed. "Gently, if you please. Tell them evidence will be provided momentarily."

Gromic scowled and shook his head, thinking nothing he could tell the agitated longshanks would have the desired effect, but he turned to head down the stairs.

The stout dwarf had barely taken two steps when Mistress Reeve sat up and called to him, one hand stretched out.

"Wait!" she exclaimed, then more softly, "I mean, please, Commander. Please, have my daughter and younger son brought up here. They need… I just don't want them lying there in the dark, afraid, and…and…"

The proud woman's voice cracked, and fresh tears welled up in her red-rimmed eyes. Mabon's arms tightened about her shoulders, and she looked at Torbjorn. A single word was all she could manage with her brittle voice as she stared at him, eyes glistening.

"Please."

The dwarf commander knew it was a potential threat. After fetching the boy, Gromic would have to stand watch below, and

Haeda would take the girl downstairs again, though the little one looked like she might contest the matter. The others were disposing of the bodies as the sun sank behind the mountains, their efforts part of the scheme Torbjorn had concocted on the fly. It would be well after dark before they returned, assuming they didn't get caught. There was a good chance they would have more visitors that night.

For the moment, such grim thoughts did him no favors, so with his shaggy head feeling as though it would bow his thick neck, the dwarf commander nodded for Gromic and Haeda to see to the woman's request.

If Crysten Reeve wanted to risk the lives of her children, Torbjorn would do what he had to. What was one more face in his nightmares after so many?

Dwarf and dwarfess descended the stairs, and mercifully, the girl followed after another look at the woman in Mabon's arms. There was something in the golden eyes watching the gore-stained woman that made Torbjorn uneasy. He refused to give it credence. Dread was to be expected when there was blood about, wasn't it?

"So, what happened?" Mabon asked, his gaze moving between his mother and Torbjorn. "Whose blood is this if it isn't hers?"

"We'll wait until your siblings join us." Torbjorn sighed, studying the woman's face. "I imagine none of us want to have to retell this story."

Crysten Reeve still hadn't mastered herself enough to speak, but she nodded emphatically. Mabon looked as though he were intent on untangling his thorny thoughts on the matter, but he kept such things to himself for the time being.

It took a fair bit of shouting by Gromic for Dillon to allow him to take Hadyn upstairs. Cerys had more than a few choice words for Haeda as she was herded up the stairs, but at last, the Reeve family was together. One look at their red-eyed mother had them all huddling about her. Torbjorn struggled to force words around the lump in his throat.

"Ugh, well," he began after a semi-effective attempt at clearing his throat. "Now that you are here, your mother wants to explain her current state, and after your curiosity is satisfied, I have a question or two of my own."

Cerys looked like she would fly into a rage, but before the words were fully formed, the young woman was stilled by her mother's hand.

The eyes of the Reeve children turned toward their mother, and Crysten lost her voice despite her best efforts.

"You know…things have b-been difficult since your father… since he died," she choked out, but it was apparent that she wouldn't last. "I… I tried my best to…to… But Gwilym changed the agreement, and then Owyn, he…"

The woman folded in on herself, and she buried her face in Mabon's chest again. The children stared at their mother, pale-faced and open-mouthed, but she continued to weep quietly against her son. Her strength had evaporated.

Torbjorn cleared his throat again and was rewarded by the pressure of three sets of inquiring eyes.

"It seems your mother secured a loan from this Gwilym, and the usurer was pressing his advantage," Torbjorn explained, reminding himself that he'd faced down a wight. A few human whelps should hardly register, yet he had to fight to keep his tone even.

"He sent someone named Owyn with a pack of ruffians to collect the debt," the dwarf commander continued. "When your mother explained the situation for our mutual benefit, we decided to…expel the debt collectors violently."

"My mother's covered in blood because you butchered men next to her?" Cerys demanded. Her brothers surveyed their mother's condition as though assessing the claim before turning narrowed eyes to the dwarf.

"We killed the men who came to hurt you and your family," Torbjorn stated. "But the blood on her came from when she… bravely fought the leader before dispatching him."

Their faces crinkled into matching expressions of incredulity before all turned toward their mother. Crysten Reeve faced her children, her face a blotchy mess and her breath coming in heaving gasps.

"I…" she began, then looked past her children to see Torbjorn give her the barest nod. "I never would have… I couldn't have done it without the commander and his men…well, his warriors, saving me in the initial attack before I…before I could find a weapon."

For the space of several heartbeats, no one spoke. Mabon's and Ceyrs' eyes wandered toward the pool of blood on the floor. Horror, disbelief, and suspicion twisted their faces, but none of them could bring themselves to ask questions or protest.

In the end, their younger brother broke the silence.

"Oh, Momma!" he murmured as he threw his arms around Crysten. "I was so scared!"

Like a spike piercing a bladder, the innocent cry robbed the other two of anything but the desire to be closer to their mother. Little brother leading the way, they enfolded the woman in a close embrace.

"I know," Crysten cried. "So was I. So was I."

The broken family clung to one another and cried. Torbjorn, despite his best efforts, looked sideways as his vision blurred. Sniffing and shaking his head, he prowled over to the fire. He tossed a few more logs onto the coals before using the poker to adjust their position. A voice in his head was screaming at him for being a sentimental fool, telling him not to take his eyes off the humans when he was outnumbered.

If this is how it ends, so be it, he told the voice. *Wouldn't be the worst way to go.*

He heard the scuff of feet on the floor; someone was

approaching his exposed back. For an eternal second, he debated letting the final stroke come—surrendering to the blow that would send him to his clan at last. He supposed the boy would use a stool since that was closest to hand, but Torbjorn thought it might be a cast iron pan, though he hoped not. Somehow it seemed nobler to die by having his skull crushed by furniture rather than cookware, though he wasn't sure why.

He heard an unhurried step closing the distance, and he heaved a sigh... but then he remembered that as weary as his heart and as blood-sick as his soul were, it wasn't just he who would pay. If they felled him, they would get his dagger and magsax, then they'd find his duabuw resting by the hearth. Would that be enough for them to lay him low?

The third and final step was falling when Torbjorn cursed himself, and with a deep swallow of air, whirled, brandishing the glowing end of the poker.

"That's close enough!" he growled before looking down the length of iron at Mabon Reeve's wide eyes.

"Oh," the young man squeaked. The cherry-red point hovered in front of his nose as he hung there frozen, one arm extended with an open hand.

The tension bled out of the dwarf commander, replaced by a bone-deep shame.

"Sorry, lad," Torbjorn muttered as he slowly lowered the poker. "Old habits and all that."

For a second, Mabon hung there, hand still out between him and the dwarf. His eyes watched the dimming point as it hovered just above the floor. Then he remembered himself, and realizing his hand had been left extended long enough, he let his arms hang at his sides as he met the dwarf commander's eyes.

"Commander Torbjorn, sir," the young man began, the first hint of a man's gravitas in his voice. "Thank you for saving my mother. You didn't have to."

"You're welcome, lad." Torbjorn thrust his chin toward

Mistress Reeve. "Now, do a paranoid old battler a favor and stand by your mother."

Mabon, a frown of disappointment flitting across his face, moved quickly to comply.

"Right then." The dwarf commander kept his gaze on them as he settled the poker beside the hearth. "We all have a better measure of each other now, but there are still a few knots that need untangling."

Reflexively, Mabon and Crysten's eyes drifted toward the floor.

"That's right," Torbjorn intoned with a dry chuckle. "We've got a bloody tunnel with something inside it that makes me bum pucker just thinking about it."

The younger two siblings appeared to be ignorant of the secret in their mother's bedroom, but the young woman didn't seem to appreciate the mention of the dwarf's posterior.

"Gross," she muttered. Her little brother stifled a giggle behind his hand.

Mabon looked at his mother before turning back to Torbjorn, hands raised as he shrugged.

"I'm sorry, but I didn't know about it until you opened it in front of me," he confessed, pointedly not turning his gaze back to his mother.

Crysten Reeve took a fortifying breath before meeting the dwarf commander's eyes.

"I don't suppose you've ever heard of Ol' Whitey, have you, Commander Torbjorn?"

CHAPTER SIXTEEN

"So, there's a demon under us, and the longshanks are saying it isn't their fault? Good one! Tell me another."

While Torbjorn was glad to see the former ranger up and about since his magical healing, he noted that Waelon's acerbic attitude had not shown any signs of improvement. The fiery-haired dwarf leaned against the far wall, watching the rear of the home while the rest of the crew, with the exception of Utyrvaul, gathered around the kitchen table. The svartalf was watching the front of the house, keeping up the annoying habit of looking so bored that he might nod off. If Torbjorn hadn't known the elf was their keenest sentry, he might have mentioned that, but it would only give the mocking myrkling another opportunity to spar verbally.

With Waelon back, it was unlikely to be settled quickly or quietly.

"Whatever's down there has been about since the Reeves took up living here." Torbjorn shrugged. "According to Crysten, rumors and tales of Ol' Whitey have been around since she was a child in the town. Word was that it came when the dwarfs came down the mountains, brought with them or summoned by them when they came to the old stones in Paeton's Watch that didn't welcome them."

A chorus of snorts and wagging heads came from the veterans at the thought of stone unfriendly to their kind. The dwarf commander noticed that only red-faced silence came from the two younger Valeborn dwarfs at the far end of the table.

"Leave it to humans," Haeda muttered. "They'll believe anything."

"As though a dwarf would bother with such kak." Waelon huffed, arms crossed over his broad chest.

"That's what I don't understand." Gromic grunted as he scooted from the table and ambled over to the pot hanging by the hearth. "Why would dwarfs truck about with a monster? What could some gribley skulker-in-the-dark do for any dwarf worthy of the name?"

There were grunts of affirmation and bobbing heads until Tomza cleared her throat. Then every eye swung her way. Gromic froze, a ladle full of stew dripping just shy of his bowl. For a moment, the young dwarfess was crushed under the weight of those stares, but Torbjorn nodded encouragingly, and she rallied.

"Well," she began, her voice thinner and reedier than usual, "if it is, and we've no reason to believe it is, but if it is a creature from the Shrieking Stair, then there's no end to the things it could do in service to its master, dwarf or otherwise. That's assuming the demon is not just a folksy flourish for something that's just a throwback or a freak."

"The Shrieking what?" Gromic asked, ladle still in hand.

"The Shrieking Stair, or what ancient humans called the Cacophonic Kingdom," Tomza replied as she shrank inward and looked at her brother. "Though, to be honest, I'm not well versed on the nature of the place. Mother seemed to think awareness of it was enough, and other things merited my attention, but Father taught Ober the outsider's lore."

The eyes all swung to the young dwarf, who didn't seem very pleased about being the center of attention. For a time, he tried to pretend there was something interesting in the last glob of stew drying at the bottom of his bowl, but Waelon was having none of it.

"Hurry up and get to gabbin', lad," Waelon growled as he stamped a boot impatiently. "The quicker we know, the quicker we can get to killin' the damned thing."

"Not sure that will do much good." Ober sighed, leaving off his bowl and looking around the room. "The things from the Stair aren't from Erduna, not like the dragons who sprang up when she was still molten and half-formed or the gods men worship when they ascend from mere mortals. Since our sacred texts speak only of Erduna's coming and future, we don't know much, but there are passages dedicated to warnings about the Stair and the sort of things that come out of it, though…well, they all come from those who follow the Speaker."

At the mention of the heretical sect, every dwarf in the room save Ober and Tomza turned and spat with near-mechanical coordination. Utyrvaul's head reared back in confusion, and he swept the room with a look of bemusement.

"My goodness, what was *that* about?" the elf demanded. "I know dwarven manners are homespun, but bodily fluids flying about seems churlish even for your sort."

"Mind your business, blade-ear," Waelon snapped.

"I'm not trying to be rude, dear," Utyrvaul retorted. "But if you're going to be launching excretions about, I need to know so that I can step clear at the next event. Now, what was that about?"

"Dwarf family business," Torbjorn said and motioned toward the front of the house. "Attend to your duties, or you'll be keeping watch from outside the door."

The svartalf didn't like the idea of standing sentinel in the cold, but his curiosity was piqued.

"Very well." He feigned a yawn. "Just thought there was something interesting for once. You know, the whole bit about a Speaker."

Again dwarven heads turned, and again spittle hit the floor. After this display, several sets of dwarven eyes glared at the myrkling, daring him to repeat his experiment.

"How curious," Utyrvaul muttered.

For a time, none spoke, though Gromic returned the ladle to the pot, having lost his appetite. He settled on the bench between Tomza and Ober while the others found a middle point to stare at. Finally, Torbjorn caught Ober's eye and nodded for him to continue. The young dwarf gave a few short coughs and carried on.

"The Shrieking Stair is a realm different from the one Erduna and the Cradle of Stars she dwells in, what we call our universe or reality. In this other-verse, the Stair or kingdom or whatever, everything descends to the lowest point in a near-eternity of sinking to where something called the Devourer or the One-Eyed King exists. I can't say it lives there because nothing in that realm really lives, not as we would call life. But that thing at the bottom feeds on everything above it that comes within reach, drawn in either by what passes for arms in that place or maybe just by the power of its presence."

All the dwarfs around Ober listened with rapt attention, barely daring to breathe, except for Tomza, who got paler with every word spoken. Torbjorn wondered at the lass' reaction. Was it fear of the idea or something more familiar that sapped her color?

"Well, the other things on the Stair are all fighting to keep from being food for the One at the bottom, clawing up and pushing others down, buying themselves more time. Sometimes the very powerful or the very lucky find places or people that allow them to cross to our world where for a time, they escape by feeding others to the One. Even the least of these intruders is terribly powerful, and because it is not born Erduna, it is not bound by the same limits as those within the Cradle of Stars."

"Bound by the same limits?" Waelon asked. "Stones and Bones, what does that mean?"

Ober opened his mouth to answer, but Tomza spoke first, her voice distant and weary.

"It means steel and iron won't kill it," the young dwarfess intoned, her shoulders bowing. "You can hurt it and distract it with the pain of injuries to the body formed around its presence here, but if it has been on Erduna as long as the Reeves say, its connection here is very strong, and a bolt to the face or a sword to the belly will just delay the inevitable when it has its terrible way with you and sends what remains to the Devourer."

Another bout of quiet fell through the room, eyes drifting to the Valeborn siblings, concern and fear behind every gaze.

"Not to be the blunt chisel here," Gromic interjected into the silence. "But I don't rightly see how my question was answered. Why, Stone preserve us, would any dwarf go about with the Erduna-forsaken spawn of such an awful place?"

"Protection," Tomza explained, the word coming out with a hint of defensiveness that only Torbjorn seemed to note. "If they were… heretics who settled here after the conquest, it would make sense that they'd want some way to make sure their secrets stayed safe. It is a common thing to barter for those services with one from the Stairs, at least among those who do such things. It doesn't matter. If that thing is down there, the likes of us would do best to leave it be."

The dwarf commander wondered at the dwarfess' tone and why she hurried on from this point.

"If it's so powerful, why is something like a bookcase stopping it?" Haeda asked. Her eyes darted down as though she expected to see evidence of the thing's return spring up from the floor.

"I suspect that area has wards and sigils of protection," Tomza said, thankful for a different question to answer. "The thing was probably curious when the passage was opened again if what Crysten told the commander is true. It can get out to prey on those in this area, so it's not really trapped. Might have just wanted to see if there were new supplicants or whatever."

"I'm not sure it does us any good to dwell on the thoughts of things like that," Ober declared, unhappy with the direction of the conversation. "The point remains the same. We keep the passage closed and try to forget it's there for all our sakes, then hoof it back to dwarvish territory right quick-like."

Several heads bobbed in agreement. Torbjorn drew confused looks when he spoke.

"I'm afraid it's not going to be that easy."

The Bad Badgers stared at their commander. Every line of his face spoke a language the veterans knew intimately and the newest additions were just becoming familiar with. What they read set all of them to muttering curses under their breath.

"Erduna's knickers." Gromic gulped. "You're talking about going down there, aren't you?"

Torbjorn traced a thumb across the burn scar on his cheek as his lips formed a grim line beneath his mustache. Before he bothered to nod, every dwarf knew the answer.

"Before Crysten's husband died, he went down into those passages," he explained, meeting every dwarf's eye to impress the significance of what he was saying on them. "He was down there for a bit before Ol' Whitey chased him out, and when he came back, after he'd had a drink or ten to settle his nerves, he told his wife about a network of tunnels that stretched out in every direction, including to the north. Talked about some of them having rails and carts like what our kind built to connect Torvgrud to Heimgrud."

The gathered dwarfs squirmed in their seats, or in the case of Waelon, shuffled from one foot to the other as though he had pebbles in his boots. Eyes darted around the room, desperate for an inspiration that would settle their nerves, though none would have dared admit it.

"I'm not going to pretend this isn't risky," their commander continued. "But given that those tunnels have exits to let the demon out to do its hunting, that seems our best bet for getting to the Pickets without being hounded by hunting parties until we're surrounded and brought down halfway across the distance we need to cover. We had to spend time recovering, so more of the wheezer's forces have swept down from the mountains to look for us, and it's only sheer dumb luck that they haven't stumbled across us here. We make for the trails heading north, and we might as well just head straight for the wight's entourage and plan to return to our clans in short order."

Everyone except Waelon approved of the idea, but when he read the room, Torbjorn could tell that none of them fancied their chances either way.

"So, it's an army we can't escape or a demon we can't beat." Haeda's chin sank down to hands folded on the table before her. "Don't see how we can win either way."

"Our little Valeborns just said we can't kill it," Torbjorn reminded, forcing himself to sound eager. "They didn't say anything about beating it."

Frowns sprang up all around.

"What's the difference?" Gromic asked, bemused.

Torbjorn looked at each dwarven face before fixing his eyes on Ober. The young dwarf felt the intensity of his stare and shook his head.

"I'm not sure if...my passenger is any match for that thing, and even then, it wouldn't be safe for the rest of you—"

Ober fell silent when Torbjorn's smile widened.

"Didn't you say your father was of the Engraver's Lodge?"

CHAPTER SEVENTEEN

"I'm pretty sure you didn't come here for rusted tools, but if it gets you badgers out of here, I'm not going to miss them."

Ober stood at the bottom of the ladder, one foot and hand bracing it as Dillon rummaged in the loft of the barn. The young dwarf allowed the slur from the salty manservant, telling himself the human was still unsettled from the events surrounding the debt collectors. He knew what it was like to wait bound and hopeless, and he wouldn't wish that on a land-stealing longshanks, or he told himself that was so.

"Hold her steady, damn you," the man snarled over his shoulder. "You'd be better off using two hands, or I'm liable to drop something on your head and make you even shorter."

Ober's grip hadn't wavered for a second, and he knew that if anything hurtled down on his head, it wouldn't be an accident. That was why his other hand was resting on his magsax and would not go anywhere no matter how the man groused.

There were more sounds of scrapping and bumping about above, interspersed with muttered curses. Dillon surreptitiously checked every so often to see if Ober's attention had waned.

Unfortunately for whatever petty scheme he was concocting, the young dwarf kept his gaze fixed on the leathery man.

"What do you need these for anyway?" Dillon asked, pausing for a heartbeat to narrow one bloodshot eye at the dwarf. "I thought you dwarfs found human tools too finicky and crude?"

Ober broke into an easy smile calculated to thwart and frustrate the surly man.

"Any exit in a cave-in, as my people say."

"That's not an answer, badger," the human growled, his shoulders tensing as he craned his neck about for a better look. "Makes me uneasy about this whole business."

"You and me both." Ober shrugged before he noted the tension in the man's posture. Ober hadn't been a soldier for long, but long enough to have developed an instinct for imminent violence. That might have had something to do with the thing sharing his body.

"How about you think real hard before you do something stupid," the young dwarf warned as the magsax rose in gleaming increments from its scabbard. "No one needs to get hurt over some chisels."

Ober's heart quickened as he saw something harden behind the man's muddy gaze.

"It's about much more than that," Dillon hissed between clenched teeth.

Ober opened his mouth to make another attempt at de-escalating the situation as the man's labor-thickened limbs bunched and flexed. Ober didn't even have time to cry out as a small iron-bound box hurtled through the air and hit him squarely in the chest. His mail took the bone-snapping force out of the ungainly projectile, but it hit hard enough to knock him on his backside as the air left his lungs. As he went down, the foot bracing the ladder kicked out, making the assemblage of pegged and lashed timber twist wildly under Dillon.

The manservant gave a wordless shout as he leapt clear of the tumbling ladder, which became a scream of pain when he came down roughly on his twisted leg. The crippled limb crumpled under him, and the man struck the hard-packed dirt floor of the barn. His outstretched hands were unable to arrest the momentum that sent him face-first into the dirt.

Ober staggered to one knee, still trying to force air into his stubborn lungs, as Dillon got up on all fours. Between them lay the chest of tools. Its rusted latch had been knocked open by its violent misuse, and spilled out an assortment of hand tools, not least of which was a mallet and a hatchet. Dwarf's and human's eyes locked over the collection of potential weapons for a single heartbeat, then both launched forward.

Ober was the first upright, but Dillon was closer and settled for scuttling crablike toward the mallet. The longshank's thick fingers closed around the rough wooden handle as Ober closed with a wide swing that sent Dillon reeling back to avoid having his jaw smashed up over his nose. With a reverse of momentum surprising in a stoutly built creature, the young dwarf dove under the man's return swing, feet pumping and shoulder lowered. Despite the difference in height, the man and dwarf were closer in weight than they might have guessed, but Dillon's bulk did him little good when Ober's lower center of gravity and traction handily upended him.

The manservant let out a startled cry before he hit the barn floor with a wounded grunt as he was smashed between armored dwarf and the unyielding earth. His head had snapped back with the impact, rebounding off the dirt, and the world spun as his eyes struggled to focus. Something stomped hard on his arm, which hurt but not as much as it should. Dillon no longer possessed his mallet. One long, wheezing breath later, he found himself looking down the length of a magsax hovering just over his eyes.

"You're a stupid man," the dwarf spat, chest heaving and gray eyes burning as he held his sword lethally steady.

"Better a man than a murderous stone-squatter!" the human snarled up the bare blade. His eyes were even redder than before, as though his hatred had manifested in a crimson glare.

The magsax inched forward, forcing Dillon to twist his head to one side to keep the point from pressing into his nose.

"It'd be so easy," Ober growled. "Just lean a little more. Put a little more weight down."

The point nestled into the man's sunken cheek, the sharp tickle of steel an icy promise of more to come.

"Do it!" Dillon snarled as he lay beneath the sword's tip. "You know I'd do the same to you. Just get it over with!"

Ober looked into the man's face, and for the blink of an eye, he saw the face twist and warp. The features settled into those of the men who burned down his home with his mother still inside. In one face, Ober saw all those who had tied his father to an apple tree the dwarf artisan had planted when he'd built the home where he would raise his family. They then shot arrow after arrow into him while he screamed. The young dwarf saw through time and space and painful memories so that every man he'd hated since that day coalesced into the one under his boot and blade.

Then he saw another face on top of his. For a single rending moment, he saw his father's face reflected in those murky eyes.

Without knowing why, he looked at the man's twisted leg. The manservant wore his scars on the outside as well as on the inside. Ober wasn't sure if that made things easier or harder.

With a deep breath, the young dwarf stepped back, magsax held firmly in his hand though it hung at his side. Dillon lay there blinking, chest heaving, and he looked at Ober, mouth slack in disbelief.

"Get up." Ober sighed. "I'll take you inside and come back. I've got everything I need." The dwarf nodded at the tools scattered across the barn floor, then pointed at the door. "Let's go."

Shuffling and struggling with his bad leg more than usual,

Dillon rose to his feet, still staring at the dwarf. Ober waited, nodding at the door when Dillon leaned against a stall post, disbelief stamped on his features.

Slowly, each step a lurching limp, Dillon made for the door. Ober walked a few steps behind him. He was halfway to the door when he stopped his hobbling advance and began to turn around.

Ober's grip tightened on the hilt of his sword, a maelstrom of contrary emotions raging inside him.

"Time to go inside," he instructed as though speaking to a young child. "Come on, now."

Dillon looked at the dwarf and then at his bare blade, and for a second, Ober thought the man was mad enough with hate to lunge for it. The young dwarf steeled himself for what he might have to do, knowing he couldn't count on luck again.

"Why?" the man asked, his voice thick.

The dwarf took a breath, opened his mouth to answer, and closed it again. How could he answer a question that had been chasing around in his head since he'd seen the reflection in Dillon's eyes?

The silence between them stretched until Ober gave a shrug and then pointed toward the house.

"Your son's in there, isn't he?"

Dillon's head rose and fell warily, fear clear on his features for the first time.

"You tell your boy stories?" Ober asked, his voice tenuous. "Like… like my da used to tell me?"

"Maybe," the manservant frowned, suspicion written on his face.

Ober forced a breath through his tightening throat.

"Stories about the war?"

"The good ones," the human replied, chin thrust forward. He met the young dwarf's eyes and admitted, "And when I'm in the cups, the bad ones."

Ober heaved another sigh as he nodded in acknowledgment of the honesty.

"Well, maybe when we're gone, you can tell him a new story," he said, his mouth dry and his chest tight. "A story that ends better than the ones about men killing dwarfs and dwarfs killing men. A story where man and dwarf...well, where they both walked away, a little wiser and both alive."

Dillon's eyes fell to the barn floor, unable to endure the gleaming gray eyes of the dwarf as he shuffled for the door.

"Aye." He grunted as he took another pained step. "That's one worth telling."

"Do you have everything you need?" Torbjorn asked as he watched the young dwarf clean the tools recovered from the barn.

"They're hardly better than the toys my father gave me when I could barely walk," Ober grunted, scouring a chisel with such force you'd have thought it offended him. "But they'll do better than hacking away with swords and axes, not that it means this idea will work."

"It'll work," Torbjorn stated with a certainty that both knew he didn't have. As though to prove it to himself and the others present at the table, he rapped his knuckles on one of the four boards collected from the barn and recently cleaned.

"Not to be a bore," Utyrvaul called from the stool in the corner, long legs stretched out before him as he sat running an oiled rag over the Reeve family sword, "but I'm not sure exactly how any of this *works*, as you so succinctly put it. What will scratchings on a few boards do to guard us against a *mallevoug*?"

"A what?" Gromic asked from the front where he kept watch, pipe in hand.

"My kind's word for a demon," the elf replied. "We have our

own body of knowledge about such things, not that anyone bothered to ask. I am admittedly not a keen student, but I don't believe I've ever heard anything about simple carvings being proof against such things."

"Perhaps they covered that at blade-ear school on a day you missed," Waelon offered, busying himself with the hatchet Ober had brought in from the barn. "Was probably between the lessons on how to be a snake-tongued scoundrel and a traitorous twat."

The dwarfs all snorted or chuckled, but none matched the svartalf's ringing peals of laughter.

"Ha-ha. Good one! Humorous alliteration, I love it. Hehe." The myrkling's voice became as flat and hard as a blade. "All jesting aside, do you really think young Master Ober, who despite his talents is no *dweommermancer*, can fashion magical glyphs to ward off a malign fiend?"

"Malign fiend?" Haeda asked as she topped the steps, having just gotten the girl to sleep. "Isn't that an oxymoron? I mean, I'm no demonologist but not sure anyone's ever heard of a malign fiend."

"You've clearly never delved the tantalizing depths of svartalf erotic literature," Utyrvaul retorted archly. Every dwarf in the room pulled a disgusted face. "But now's not the time for that sort of sordid luxury. I'm more concerned about the part where we hurtle through the dilapidated tunnels in a ramshackle cart, trusting roughly chiseled boards to keep the enemy at bay."

Dwarvish voices rose in outrage at the flurry of insults their kind had just endured.

"Dilapidated?" Gromic demanded.

"Ramshackle?" Waelon snarled.

"Roughly chiseled!" Ober cried the loudest.

The strength of the response left the elf's gaze darting from one scowling expression to the next as he left off tending the sword laid across his lap. He began to speak, then paused, certain that how he phrased his next words might determine whether he'd be left to fend for himself from here on out.

"My apologies," he began delicately. "It was an assumption—an admittedly ignorant one—that the underground network would be in sore shape due to many long years of disuse. Time can be unkind to even the finest craftsmanship, don't you know."

Keen to have a legitimate matter about which to criticize the myrkling, Waelon raised his chin and looked down his broad nose at Utyrvaul.

"Then you don't know what craftsmanship is, long ears," the former ranger declared to the affirming nods of his peers. "Dwarven-worked structures and dwarven-wrought machines are made to last centuries with little to no maintenance, and with a little care and diligence, they can last far beyond that. Simply put, elves were fashioned by Erduna to last for a long time, but things fashioned by dwarfs are made to last forever."

The hearty cheers of agreement drove the elf to raise his hand in surrender and put on his best ameliorating smile.

"I sit awed and corrected, of course," he wheedled, squirming on the stool as he began to work the rag over the sword again. "But I'm afraid my question remains unanswered."

"Your apology is incomplete as well," Torbjorn declared, clapping a hand on Ober's shoulder. "I've every confidence that Ober's work will be exemplary, but for all that, it will be a family effort that sees this done."

Utyrvaul's fine silver eyebrows rose as his eyes swung toward Tomza. The dwarfess refused to wilt under the crimson gaze, but her cheeks were nearly the same shade.

"So, our resident enchantress shall fill the grooves her brother so artfully hews." The myrkling nodded sagely, leaning forward as though he were in a conspiratorial conversation. "Tell me, my dear, how many times have you used your magical arts to empower wards to drive off magically potent hostile aggressors?"

Tomza glared at the svartalf but could not immediately reply.

"I don't need an exact number," the myrkling conceded. "Just a rough estimate to allay my concerns."

She swallowed, refusing to release the elf's gaze even as she muttered the only answer she could honestly give. "Never."

The silence that followed the answer hung thick and stifling in the air.

"Ah, yes." Utyrvaul sighed. "I was afraid of that."

"Do you have a better suggestion, elf?" Torbjorn growled.

The svartalf raised a long finger to his lips, brow furrowed in concentration.

"I don't suppose you'd consider me taking that gray mare and riding for help to be a viable option," he mused. He gave a surrendering shake of his head. "No, I don't suppose you would, though to be fair, Commander, I've contributed quite a bit to this operation, especially considering how late in the game I arrived. I mean, if it weren't for me, we wouldn't have this roof over our head or those demon-infested tunnels under our feet."

The dwarf commander shook his head as dwarven scowls shot toward the blissfully unfazed elf.

"Be that as it may," Torbjorn replied with monumental patience, "do you know what a dwarf calls jawing about problems without offering solutions?"

Utyrvaul raised his hand as though he had hit on an idea. "Being a productive and valued member of a team?"

"Whining," Torbjorn declared. "The plan is the plan, and we're sticking to it. While we're at it, it's a good thing you are cleaning that blade since I've got a plan for it, too."

CHAPTER EIGHTEEN

"All right, I appreciate the patience you've all exhibited during this trying time, but I'm glad to say it is nearly at an end."

The humans of the Reeve household were crammed to one side of the ground floor. Their unlooked-for houseguests were arrayed across from them. The expressions of all in the room were a mixture of relief and discomfort. None wanted to look the others in the eye, but none were so cowed as to stare at the floor, which had recently been scoured of blood and other signs of violence.

"It hasn't been easy, and if there had been any other way, I would have taken it," Torbjorn continued, meeting the eyes of those across from him. "But despite the odds, we've managed to help each other through this time in our own ways, so I hope we can now understand and trust one another."

There were shuffling and half-formed sounds from the human side of the room, and Torbjorn waited for them to settle without comment.

"So, as the first gesture of this newly formed bond, I had you all released and brought up here," the dwarf commander said with an expansive gesture. "We have nothing to fear from each other, so there is no longer any need for you to be captives in your own home."

For several heartbeats, there was no reply, then Mistress Reeve cleared her throat and nodded stiffly at the dwarf.

"Yes, thank you, Commander Torbjorn," she intoned, her voice still hoarse from the screaming and crying she'd done after the encounter with the debt collectors. "I appreciate this respectful gesture toward my family."

Torbjorn nodded graciously and motioned with one hand for Utyrvaul to step forward. The elf's usually graceful movements were ungainly as he stepped toward the Reeve family, sword held rigidly before him. If the svartalf's expression was any indication, he was on the verge of being ill.

"As a further indication of our goodwill and trust," the dwarf commander explained, sweeping an open hand toward Mabon, "we would like to return this sword to your family. Among our people such things are sacred, so I would not have it depart the bloodline it is bound to. May you bear it with honor."

The young man took a step toward the elf who loomed over him, teeth bared in what could only technically be called a smile. The elder Reeve son gripped the hilt and scabbard, but he had to give a hearty tug before the elf released the weapon. Utyrvaul stepped back with pained slowness, a wistful look on his face as his red eyes followed the engraved mammoth-tusk hilt.

"Thank you," Mabon intoned as he attached the scabbarded blade to his belt. "I know you didn't have to—"

"In the endeavor of bearing the blade with honor," Torbjorn interjected, his expression hardening, "I trust that you will be honored to bear the weapon beside us as we venture through the tunnels together."

There was a catch in the collective breath of the humans. Every dwarf tensed as though expecting violence to explode. Beneath the pleasant expression on Torbjorn's face, bile bubbled at the back of his throat. He had nearly choked on the words, but now they were out, and he was bound by them. He could see no other way.

A wise, smarter dwarf might've been better suited for this, he thought as he waited for the response of the Reeve household. *But Stone and Bones, I'm the one who's here, so we'll have to make do.*

Fittingly, Crysten Reeve was the first to find her voice.

"So, my elder son will join you in your travel through the tunnels?" the matron asked, her eyes a glassy mask. "That is what I am to understand?"

Before Torbjorn could so much as nod, several human voices rose in protest. Cerys' shrill demand cut through clear and sharp.

"Why the hell would he do that?"

Torbjorn took heart when he saw her mother grip the young woman's arm. She hated it, of course, but the matriarch of the home understood. Like warring kings meeting over a carnage-strewn field of battle, a battle neither could win which might destroy both, dwarf and woman locked eyes, and an understanding passed between them. Torbjorn hoped the full extent of his distaste and disgust for this whole matter had been conveyed, but regardless, the bargain had been struck.

To throw the poor mother a bone, Torbjorn turned to meet the horrified eyes of the young woman.

"Because, lassie, by all rights, your brother should be dead," the commander stated. "He was taken captive, which is no sin, but then he directed us to your home and helped negotiate our sheltering here. While here, we've used your home to hide from forces allied with your current liege, and your home has harbored enemy warriors."

Cerys looked at her brother, whose cheeks were burning with shame. To his credit, he refused to lower his face even as tears began to stream down his cheeks. Torbjorn imagined that with time and guidance, he would have made a good soldier, maybe even a good officer. He had a strength that his capture and humiliation hadn't beaten out of him, and that was no small thing.

Too bad he ran across us.

"He didn't have a choice," Cerys shouted, her gaze darting from the dwarf to her brother and back. "If he hadn't done what you said, what you told him to do, you would have killed him."

Torbjorn heard the tremble in the young woman's voice and refused to harden himself against it as he held her stare.

"Then his masters would have expected him to die." The commander sighed wearily. "A soldier's life is the coin spent by those he serves. He hopes it is not spent wastefully, but he cannot rally to the banner and expect he will not be called upon to pay the price."

Cerys ripped free of her mother's grip and stepped forward to stab an accusing finger at Torbjorn.

"Coins and prices!" she shrieked. "You're talking about *lives*! You're talking about my brother's life!"

"Not just your brother's," the dwarf replied, his tone even and unhurried. "I'm talking about my life and the life of every dwarf under my command, and even that fool of an elf. I'm talking about every soldier, dwarf or man, goblin or elf, every last creature of Erduna who has taken up arms to fight for king, country, or gods. It is the hard commerce of war on this ruined world."

Out of the corner of his eye, Torbjorn saw something strange pass over Dillon's face, and the man's dark eyes darted toward Ober. The dwarf commander wondered what had passed between the two in the barn that merited the look, but then the young woman's voice drew him back to the inescapable tragedy before him.

"But why take *him*? What do you need him for?" she pressed, her voice softening as he saw the wheels turning behind her eyes. Even before he could give an answer, she was fomenting arguments and weighing lines of rebuttal.

"First, it is to assure that there are no more surprises when we enter the tunnels," the commander put forth, determined to keep his voice steady and low. "To give her son the best chance of surviving, your mother will make sure we know all that there is to know about the tunnels."

Cerys' eyes shot to her mother, both pleading and accusing as the woman stood silent and still.

"Second, it will keep anyone from telling your masters where we are and where we are headed," Torbjorn continued. "If the wight's forces find us, assuming they don't kill him at the outset when they attack, he will be brought back and executed as a traitor. We've made certain of it by placing dwarvish coins among the dead debt collectors. It will look like he attempted to pay them with dwarvish coins, and when they demanded more, he had his dwarvish friends kill them before seeking sanctuary with us."

Muttered oaths and curses greeted the explanation.

"If they do not find us, they will have no connection between Mabon and us," Torbjorn went on. "Indeed, it makes it seem as though Gwilym or his associates had dealings with dwarfs that went poorly. I imagine the usurer is not very popular, so once the finger is pointed, there will be plenty of debtors eager to turn suspicion to certainty. With any luck, he'll be swinging from a rope not long after they find his dead thugs."

The angry profanity had ceased, and there was hopeful light in Crysten's eyes at the thought. Torbjorn was determined to finish this conversation, so he pressed on.

"Third and finally, it is the best chance your brother has to stay alive and have your family name unsullied," he declared in a tone that brooked no further argument. "If he comes with us, it is not as a prisoner but as a hired sword, a mercenary like Utyrvaul. When we reach the dwarvish lands, he will be welcome to travel with us until we no longer have need of him or he finds some other opportunity to make his way that's more to his liking."

Torbjorn turned to look Mabon in the eye, the dwarf's dark, burning gaze refusing to let the young man look away.

"To dwarvish territory, and then your life is your own," Torbjorn said, each word as heavy and hard as an ingot. "Make your fortune in the wider world or bide your time and return home; the choice is yours. Who knows? You humans count years differently than our kind, and much can change in a few of Erduna's circuits. With time and some luck, you could return home a wealthy man to a hero's welcome."

Mabon swallowed and the beet-red color left his cheeks. "Or not return." He gulped, his knuckles standing out white as they gripped his belt as though it and the sword it once more carried might flee.

"Perhaps." The dwarf nodded slowly. "We cannot return home until we are dead, so we call death 'returning to our clan.' If that helps you face what lies ahead, you are welcome to think of it that way free of charge. Never thought you'd hear a dwarf say that, eh?"

The lad didn't laugh at the joke, but something hard and certain formed behind the watery stare, and his body let go of its tension.

There it is. The commander chuckled internally. *Lad's got iron there, even if he's just a weedy longshanks.*

"Can I have a moment to say goodbye?" Mabon asked, his voice stronger and deeper than it had been before.

Torbjorn blinked back something prickling in the corner of one eye. "Aye, lad." He grunted thickly.

"We can make time for that."

"Part of me hates you," Crysten Reeve admitted. She was standing in her room, one hand raised over the stone which would open the bookcase. "You are taking a piece of my heart away, and you've assured me that it will be years before I see it returned."

Torbjorn nodded, having no rebuttal to her statement.

He looked at the dwarfs assembling in preparation for entering the tunnel. At the fore stood Gromic and Waelon, forming an armored bulwark of dwarvish meat behind shields bearing two of the ensorcelled planks. Both had their duabuws resting on the rims of their shields, ready to fire, though they only had a bolt a piece. Behind them was the gap where Torbjorn would stand, then Haeda, the girl, and Mabon. Contrary to her usual sanguinity, the golden-eyed child stared at the bookcase as though she knew what lay ahead. Behind them stood Utyrvaul, as inscrutably flippant as ever. His red eyes made a lazy pass over the procession. At the rear stood the Valeborn siblings, their shields bearing the other two graven planks.

It was as strong a formation as they could compose that gave them any hope of warding off the foul denizen within the tunnels.

"But I am also deeply thankful for you," Mistress Reeve continued, drawing the dwarf commander's attention to her once more. "More than once, you've shown mercy when you did not have to, and even now, you are still giving us a chance, however small, for a reunion we have no right to."

Torbjorn didn't have the attention to spare to be embarrassed, but he bowed his head to the woman.

"One day." He grunted as he picked up his shield and shouldered his duabuw. "I hope to return this way and perhaps see you ride your fine horse as you take me to see Paelon's Watch. I doubt I will live to see that day, but it doesn't hurt to hope."

The woman's head moved slowly from side to side.

"Oh, no, Torbjorn," she whispered, her voice tight and hoarse. "Nothing hurts more than hope, but it is pain which sustains. It will sustain me until Mabon is returned to me, and maybe it can sustain you until that day."

Torbjorn smiled, bowed his head once more, and moved to take his place.

"Watchman keep you," Crysten called as she pressed the corner of the stone. "All of you."

There was grinding within the stone, and as the bookcase slid back, the tunnel yawned open.

From above came the uneven thump of ungainly feet making for the steps.

"Crysten!" Dillon called. "Crysten! Soldiers! Soldiers, and there's a wight with 'em!"

As the assembly moved into the tunnel, Torbjorn's heart leapt into his throat, and his gaze snapped to the matron of the Reeve family. He saw the tension in her body and the fear and anger in her eyes. For one awful moment, the dwarf was certain it was all for naught.

They all heard a fist hammering on the door.

Dwarf's and woman's eyes met for the last time.

"Hurry," she hissed, hand trembling over the tilted stone.

A heartbeat later, they trudged into the tunnel. The gears rumbled, and the bookcase shot back into place.

In the darkness beyond, a thin voice laughed.

CHAPTER NINETEEN

None spoke, but the lanterns were lit without a command being given.

No sooner had they been lit than all gaped at the figure before them.

That which was named Ol' Whitey, true to its name, was a pale creature with skin between chalk and curdled milk. The cadaverous covering was stretched taut over a spindly frame except about the throat and belly, where it hung in pendulous folds. Another strained, wispy laugh rose from the creature, setting the drooping flesh wobbling as its thin lips peeled back from rows of glistening black teeth. Wet, filmy eyes the color of hematomas bulged out of the thin face over that hideous mouth, crinkling around the weeping edges to complete the impression of mad mirth.

The anemic, sawing laugh grew as it approached, and if not for the raw terror its advance produced, the gathering might have feared the enemies they'd so recently fled would hear. However, such was the soul-striking horror of the thing that wore this form like a garment that neither dwarf nor human nor elf could bring themselves to move or even think. The malign presence came for them, and not a bolt was fired or a blade drawn.

One knobby paw stretched out to pluck Gromic like the first plump morsel at a feast. The stout dwarf's blue eyes filled with tears as his mouth slid open. No scream came forth as a clawed fingertip made to caress the brow of his helmet. There was the cry of metal parting unwillingly, and every soul waited to see Gromic's end come with mocking ease. Then a fresh light that had nothing to do with lanterns rose from the dwarf's shield.

To call it a flash was to give it more physicality than it possessed. For a staggering instant, there was illumination where there had been none, then it was gone. Amid the dancing after-images, everyone saw Ol' Whitey recoil, its gnarled limb smoking and blackened as if it had held it in a fire.

The event shattered the hold the fiendish being had over them, and as Ol' Whitey began to retreat, the dwarvish reply came. Bolts hissed through the air, but the demon twisted with boneless grace, letting the projectiles sing by. Ol' Whitey's bruised gaze followed their trajectory with rapt attention before it snarled at the temerity of the dwarfs who had fired upon it.

Then the thing drew itself up to its full height and stood taller still, mottled flesh stretching and straining. Its limbs resembled poles tipped with grasping spiders, one still pale, the other charred, and its mouth formed a yawning pit ringed with black teeth. It seemed like the demon could gather them all up with one scoop before it drove them one after the other into a mouth as hungry as the grave.

But the dwarfs were no creature's meal, not without a fight, so with shoulders behind their shields, the front line of the Bad Badgers advanced. Ol' Whitey jeered, but as the plank-hung shields closed, that arrogance disappeared. For the first time in a long time, Ol' Whitey retreated, balking at these peculiar visitors to its domain. Overlong limbs writhed as it squirmed back up the tunnel.

None chased the thing into the dark, but a wheedling voice moaned into their minds.

Not fair, not fair, not fair.

Then not even its crooked fingers could be seen, and silence reigned once more. The rasp of heavy breathing registered, and each was certain their hammering heartbeats were audible to all. Another moment passed, and their breathing and the thunder of their hearts slowed, but none seemed able to speak. What could be said in the face of what they'd just seen and experienced?

Torbjorn found the answer. "Forward."

Their bodies responding to the authority in the command, all trudged forward. In a tight formation, they quickened their pace, and it seemed the drive to run would win out and their little victory would be lost.

Again, the commander's voice rang out when needed. "Steady."

Like a tiny rudder steering a great ship, the word arrested the accelerating steps of the crew, and for some time, they jogged down the tunnel. Eyes darted around, chasing every recoiling shadow as they went. Ol' Whitey seemed to have surrendered this section of the tunnels to them. For several minutes, there was nothing but the rattle of their gear and armor and the tromping of their feet. The lanterns revealed only bare stone.

Then, without warning, the tunnel walls were gone, and they hurtled into a wide chamber. Torbjorn fought to force the command from his throat.

"Reform."

Gromic kept the forward position. Waelon shifted to shuffle crablike to the right while Tomza rushed to the left. At their heels, Ober's head swiveled this way and that, his board-bearing shield ready to intercept.

"Not long now," Torbjorn called in a voice that echoed around the chamber. His eyes strained in the lantern light. Crysten had told him this chamber was at the end of the tunnel and said that at its far side were the carts that would carry them, Shaper willing, northward along the ancient rails. Perhaps she had been led to believe this chamber was smaller? In his terrified flight from the fiend hunting the Bad Badgers, had Reeve wrongly estimated the size when recounting the tale to his wife?

Torbjorn knew their reformed positions were weak and the number of shield bearers was insufficient to guard them effectively. He'd counted on the fiend's confusion and hesitancy to cover the distance, but he'd not reckoned with the size of the room, which might have been crossed far faster on human legs than dwarven ones. But they were in motion, and there was nothing they could do.

"Faster," Torbjorn growled as though sheer force of will could hold them in formation as their pace quickened.

Behind him, Haeda had scooped up the girl. Mabon puffed and sweated from fear or effort; it was hard to tell.

The lantern light picked out the steep sides of the cart as Ober gave a cry.

Moving across the ceiling spiderlike without sacrificing an ounce of speed, Ol' Whitey skittered overhead. With its good hand, it smashed the young dwarf to the stone with a strength at odds with the emaciated limb that delivered the blow. Mail rasped on stone, and the nasal guard of the Ober's helmet gave a shriek as it kept his face from meeting the floor. Arms splayed as much by instinct as in the hope of catching himself, he had little leverage when the burned hand tore the shield from his grip.

For its shield-stripping efforts, the demon's wounded limb caught fire, and as if there had been a lightning flash, everything in the chamber stood out in glaring contrast as unhallowed flesh burned with blue-white flames. Then the shield and its plank clattered to the ground, and the comparatively dim lanterns were all that was left to illuminate the scene.

"Ober!" Tomza cried as Ol' Whitey loomed over her brother,

its mouth opening as the sagging throat and stomach wobbled in anticipation.

A roar tore from the stricken dwarf as he surged to his feet. He threw Ol' Whitey backward, limbs curling and tangling like a tumbling spider's. Ober stalked forward, stripping off helmet and sword belt as he strode, body swelling and thick dark fur erupting across his face and hands. The gray eyes became dark pools that flashed with amber light, and a voice that was not the young dwarf's rumbled out in challenge.

"Soul maggot, worm of the void!" it snarled, the words mangled as fangs crowded out teeth in the reforming face. "Let me taste your bitter blood!"

With the boneless agility that made their stomachs churn, the demon found its feet, and for a moment, it stood poised to flee. Then a queer light came into its eyes, and the slanted nostrils quivered. The drooping cavern of black fangs that was its mouth found corners to curl upward, and with that abominable grin, its thoughts slithered through every mind present.

Not yet, wyldling. So close, but not yet. Mayhaps I can help.

The links of Ober's mail strained and burst as he advanced, his hands dagger-clawed paws. With every step, he grew; soon he would erupt from the binding armor, filling the lantern light with his hairy bulk. His face was dominated by a gaping muzzle full of ivory fangs. With a guttural chuff, he sprang forward.

Bearish claws found flesh, tearing great rents in the sagging paunch before ripping upward to gouge and scrape the gray bones beneath. How could any creature bear the wounds and not expire? It seemed to be proof of the monster's deathless nature.

Ober was not to be denied, though. He drove Ol' Whitey to the stone floor with such force that it cracked and shifted under him. Rather than fight the mauling, the fiend accepted his attacker into a long-limbed embrace that coiled about the humped shoulders that bunched and strained to grind its body to powder.

Those gangly hands that caressed the pelted hulk spread wide before sinking into mail and flesh as if it were clay. Ober howled, but the sound was cut short, leaving only a faint wheeze. A spiny laugh rose from Ol' Whitey as it climbed to its feet, looming large as Ober shrank. Hands drove deeper, and the young dwarf gave a choking rattle as his fur vanished into his colorless skin.

A heartbeat later, Ober was on his hands and knees, gray eyes bulging as his mouth gaped. Like an arachnid slowly reeling in its prey, the demon's hands wound up and away from the dwarf's bowed back. Crackling arcs of amber and scarlet fire wrapped around the curling claws. From within the swirling energies came the distant groan of a wounded bear as the collection of red and gold light was drawn toward Ol' Whitey's gaping mouth.

Black teeth quivered and dripped milky saliva that glistened in the oncoming light of the plundered essence. Ober, still on his knees, stretched out a pleading hand.

"Don't," the dwarf croaked, the effort of reaching out seeming too much as he collapsed. The demon gave a vibrato chuckle, but it was not the only one affected by the young dwarf's plea.

The gripping spell of the demon gone, two dwarvish bolts punched into the mouth, sending a rush of bilious ichor gushing over black fangs. Ol' Whitey gave an angry hiss and a freshly sharpened hatchet spun through the air to carve a deep notch between its eyes. The fiend's outstretched hands flexed and curled inward, and its legs buckled, then with a rush of air like the belch of a slaughterhouse, it collapsed bonelessly to the floor.

The coruscating amalgam of scarlet and amber twisted in midair and retreated into Ober's body. The young dwarf gasped and rolled onto his side, gagging and retching. Tomza reached her brother's side first and held his head as he fought to clear the viscous froth from his throat and lungs. Gromic and Waelon hoisted him up as they raised their shields toward the fallen demon.

"To the cart!" Torbjorn shouted, working the lever on his duabuw. "Now!"

The crew sprang to action. Mabon helped Haeda pop the girl into the steep-sided cart before helping the dwarfess in. The young man was assisted by Utyrvaul, who joined him an instant later. The elf held his hand out to the first dwarf to come near. As a result, he received Ober as he was brought over, though Mabon was quick to assist the young dwarf. A heartbeat later, Tomza and Torbjorn appeared. Gromic and Waelon set their hands to the cart and began to push.

"I think we should hurry," the svartalf declared as he pointed a long finger. At the edge of the lantern light, Ol' Whitey's form stirred, one arm reaching with a marionette's awkward movements toward its slack face, from which bolt shafts and hatchet handle protruded.

"You could damn well feel free to hop out and help," Waelon snarled as he and Gromic heaved against the unyielding cart.

"Are the wheels rusted to the tracks?" Mabon asked, leaning over the edge to check.

"It's dwarvish-made," Torbjorn growled as his gaze swung to the front of the cart. "It won't rust."

A few strides ahead of them, the lantern light revealed the descending track that would send them rolling northward. Why wouldn't the bloody thing move?

A glance at the demon revealed that it had plucked the hatchet from its head and was applying a hand to each bolt. Torbjorn could have sworn he saw a wicked gleam in one rolling eye. He knew the fiend was toying with them. They might have caught it by surprise when they broke free of its paralyzing presence. Now it was savoring their panic as they desperately tried to get away.

"Erduna's dirty nethers," the commander swore as he made to join his two dwan. He found a hand gripping his shoulder firmly.

Torbjorn's eyes followed the dark hand to the myrkling's grinning face.

"One moment, Commander," he purred, leaning over the far side of the cart. "Work smarter, not harder."

Torbjorn would have screamed recriminations, but he saw the lever the elf was gripping rising from the cart's side. Utyrvaul thrust the lever forward, and with a dull *clunk*, the cart gave a lurch and began to roll.

"Gromic, Waelon!" Torbjorn shouted as his gaze swung toward Ol' Whitey to find it on its feet looking at him. "Get your arses up here *now*!"

Legs pumping and boots thumping, the burly dwans sprang up to seize the back edge before the cart plunged downward. Gromic and Waelon scrambled over the lip, aided by Torbjorn and Mabon, and spilled into the cart. In their efforts to increase its speed, they had caused a shift in the cart's direction, and as it tipped over the edge, a sliding click indicated that it had changed tracks.

All felt the shudder and shift of the cart adjusting to the new course as it rocketed down into the dark.

CHAPTER TWENTY

The cart shot down the slope, accelerating until it was all any of them could do to brace themselves against the mounting pressure. They soared down the rails, the lantern light providing glimpses of odd carvings and reliefs engraved on the walls. For all the strangeness, the passengers hardly paid them any heed, their attention either forward, behind, or within the cart.

"How is he?" Torbjorn shouted over the thrum of the wheels.

"I don't know," Tomza replied as she cradled her limp brother's head in her lap. "He's breathing normally and he doesn't have any outward signs of injury, yet I can't wake him."

"Can't you just witch him awake?" Waelon asked, frowning at the stricken dwarf.

"Not without knowing what's wrong," Tomza answered, shaking her head. "I might make whatever happened to him worse."

"How deep does this go?" Utyrvaul cried, squinting into the dark. He sounded more than a little unnerved.

"As long as it gets us clear of that thing," Haeda responded with a worried look back up the shaft gripping the girl tight to her side. The child, for her part, seemed to have forgotten the horror of the demon in the rush of the wind through her hair. If not for the dwarfess' restraining arm, she might have thrown her hands in the air.

"I hoped it was dead," Gromic said. "What are you supposed to do when a thing don't have the decency to die after getting a skullful of dwarvish steel?"

"Run," Torbjorn replied, just loud enough to be heard. "Which was why that's what we did."

"Oh, finally," Utyrvaul declared when the pitch of the slope changed and the cart slowed. A few heartbeats later, the cart gave a slight jolt. Everyone managed to keep their feet as the vehicle began to roll along a track that was nearly level.

No longer having the air whipping past them at stinging speed, all could smell the dusty age in the tunnel. It clung to the nostrils, and if one thought about it too long, it made it seem hard to breathe with the weight of it.

"These aren't dwarvish tunnels," one of the dwarfs said, but none of them knew who had said it. "At least not now."

"What do you mean?" Utyrvaul hissed in an atypical show of temper. "Are you telling me all that nonsense about no rust on the carts and the rails was bunk?"

"The rails and cart are of dwarven make," Torbjorn assured him. Something prickled at the edge of his senses, frustratingly elusive. "But this tunnel isn't. Dwarfs came after and laid the rail to explore it, but the stonework is all wrong. Dwarf tunnels are contoured to the earth, and—"

"And don't have that," Gromic wheezed as he pointed a thick finger upward.

Eyes roved after the finger, and for the first time, they examined the reliefs carved into the ceiling above them. All within the cart repressed shudders. Figures flowed across the graven stone, their bodies and faces imitations of things which, if seen in the flesh, would have made Ol' Whitey seem tame. Abominations of flesh, bone, and viscous vitality, the sculpted horrors grappled and ravaged each other and tiny pitiful figures that might have been mortal creatures who crawled away in dread. Looking on from behind and above the horrors, their ranks forming the backdrop, were impossibly tall figures, their dark faces blank except for eyes that gleamed gold in the lantern light.

Slowly but inexorably, the dwarvish eyes swung toward the golden-eyed child who huddled next to Haeda. The girl, who had been looking at the carvings with a bemused frown, felt the weight of their stares and buried her face in Haeda's side as though trying to hide the gleaming evidence in her face.

"You think these might be what's left of her people?" Tomza asked, tearing her eyes away from the cowering child to look at the other dwarfs. "I mean, there's something about the way the stones are cut that seems like what we found next to the Tooth."

None spoke, the implications as terrible as the squirming desecrations overhead. Haeda finally squeezed the girl's shoulder, then cleared her throat and faced the others with a defiant glare.

"That's impossible." She snorted, daring them to contest the point. "Nothing like this has been seen in the Vale for generations, and she's little more than a babe. It's just a coincidence."

Before the dwarfess' baleful glare, the other dwarfs balked, muttering and studying the cart beneath their feet. The young human in their midst was not as readily cowed, perhaps due to blissful ignorance rather than courage.

"I'm not sure about this Tooth business," he began, blind to the warning glances of the dwarfs next to him. "But my father always said the Vale is a big place full of strange and dangerous things. I don't expect it would be impossible for her family to have hidden in a small corner of the Vale, the last of the people who built this…place."

"Or that some form of sorcery was involved," Utyrvaul offered blithely. "After all, the likes of creatures who could summon *mallevoug* to do their bidding wouldn't bat an eye at engaging in the kind of magics necessary to preserve a life. Of course, it raises the question of why *her* life was worth the effort?"

"I don't like your tone, myrkling," the driver snarled as she rounded on the elf. "You're making a lot of assumptions that are liable to get that sharp tongue carved out."

"Wait," Gromic interrupted, heavy brows knitting. "I thought we said the Valeborn heretics were the ones who summoned Ol' Whitey?"

"Clearly, whoever who constructed these tunnels was familiar with the sort of horrors that spawn from the Cacophonic Kingdom," the svartalf replied, one long finger stabbing toward the ceiling reliefs. "And it has already been agreed upon that these passages are not of dwarf make. Therefore…"

The silence that yawned after that was prickly and uncomfortable. Haeda fought through the discomfort to offer more rebuttals.

"That may be, but it's got nothing to do with the girl," the dwarfess doggedly persisted. "And even if by some cruel fluke this was her people's long-forgotten past, she can't be blamed for it, nor will staring at the poor thing do us one bit of good."

"You're right on both counts, Haeda," Torbjorn announced, looking around the group, with a particularly pointed look at Utyrvaul. "What we need to do is figure out where this is taking us since I'm fairly certain we managed to get on the wrong track when we ran away from the demon."

There were reluctant nods, though the elf only managed an arched eyebrow before heaving a low sigh and looking away.

"We're still going northward," Waelon offered as he scrunched his nose. "But I reckon we're something like two miles deep. That means the only way we're getting out of here without a long, dangerous climb is if there's a winch at the other end."

"Well, I don't imagine they ran all this rail down here without putting one in," the dwarf commander mused, chewing the inside of his lip. "But we better be ready for either option. Though if I remember my topography, going northward slopes into a sort of trough before the Pickets. With any luck, that's where we'll come out."

"Since when have we been lucky?" came a thick-throated reply from the bottom of the cart.

"Ober!" Tomza cried. "Take it easy! You might be—"

"Thirsty." The young dwarf coughed as he unceremoniously sat up and groped for the waterskin hanging from his pack.

"Good to have you back, lad," Gromic declared with feeling as he thumped Ober's back before a glare from Tomza drove him away.

"How are you feeling, Dwan?" Torbjorn asked, not able to keep the smile from tugging at the corners of his mouth.

The young dwarf gasped after an impressive draw from the skin. "Alive and kickin', sir. I don't suppose anyone knows what happened to me."

Eyes darted around, but the silent consensus was that none of them knew how to answer the question. The silence held for another beat, then an irritated sniff issued from the elf staring down the track.

"The fiend," Utyrvaul began, refusing to turn away from his vigil, "was not satisfied with devouring your flesh, and it made a play to devour your wild spirit. I'm sure your vital essence was plucked up with the feral soul before the distraction of bodily harm broke the demon's concentration."

"Wild spirit?" Mabon asked, looking about the gathering of dwarfs. "Is that why he—"

"Not now, lad," Gromic warned with a shake of his head.

"You knew what was wrong with him all this time?" Tomza growled. She shot to her feet, one square finger jabbing at the elf. "I was terrified that he was never going to wake up, and you couldn't spare a word to tell me what had happened?"

"First, no one deigned to ask me, good lady," the svartalf replied, turning a blank stare on her. "Second, knowing what had happened meant I knew there was nothing any of us could do. The binding of his and wild thing's spirit to his body meant your brother would either recover, or the connection was so damaged that the paired souls would depart, and he would expire. Either way—"

"Either way," Ober interjected with a grunt as he dragged himself to his feet, one hand clasping his sister's shoulder. "I'm glad to be back and glad for the knowledge of what happened. Explains why I can't feel...*him* quite so much right now. I think the attack took it out of him."

"Doubtless," Utyrvaul remarked. "I imagine its will alone kept you from death."

"Don't count on it," Tomza shot back angrily. "He comes from sterner stock than you know."

"Indubitably," the elf said with another dry sniff before turning back toward the tunnel before them. "In the interest of sharing facts that none can control, our tunnel will soon be opening into a far larger space."

"How much larger?" Torbjorn asked as he shouldered his way to the front of the cart, hoisting a lantern.

"Far," Utyrvaul drawled as he leaned against the side of the cart, arms crossed.

The dwarf commander might have offered rebuke for the elf's petulant behavior, but then the tunnel walls fell away, and he was struck dumb with fresh horror and wonder.

"Shaper," Waelon groaned.

"Watchman preserve me," Mabon muttered.

The chamber they'd entered was beyond the subterranean dwarfs' ability to describe. In their own tongue, they had terms for spaces from the smallest alcove where a single dwarf might make a crude shelter to grand caverns that could house fortresses, but this was on a scope and scale never imagined. The rail drew them past a vista lit by a pale phosphorescent lake that stretched away from them for what must have been miles. The ceiling hundreds or thousands of feet above was lost in shadow. This space could swallow the grandest city known to mortals and elves and still have room for a few villages or townships.

Such a titanic space, only matched by the plunging shaft of the Deeping, would have been staggering enough, but the lord of all caverns was not empty.

Thrusting up from the gleaming waters were structures whose scale beggared the mind. Some were cyclopean spears of stone, their jagged tips like chipped fangs. Massive structures appeared to have suffered catastrophic damage and fetched up against other leaning edifices. Some of the structures had fallen over the barreled circles of what must have been immense towers that arched out of the water. Softly rippling glows playing across ruined artificial grottos.

On and on, the cart rolled on, the wheels' whispers swallowed by the soft sighs of the water's undulating breath.

"If I hadn't seen this with my own eyes, I would never have believed it was possible even for our ancestors." Torbjorn gulped, his face pale and his voice raw. "Who were these people?"

For a time, all within the cart pondered the awful question. Then Mabon's voice sounded, small and tremulous.

"I...I don't *know* anything," he asserted, licking his lips with a dry tongue. "But in some of our oldest stories and songs, the sort even our elders only know a few lines of, we have tales of sea giants coming to the Vale and oppressing the first peoples. We always thought it was silly since the Caged Sea is hundreds of miles away, and that's the closest one. We wondered why watery giants would come so far to pick on our ancestors, but maybe this was the sea they were talking about...an underground sea sitting beneath our feet all this time."

"Thinking about how big those buildings were makes my head hurt," Waelon began, scowling at the ruins. "But that tunnel we passed through isn't fit for any giant I've seen or heard of to pass through. High-roofed enough to fit the likes of one of you long-shanked humans or an elf maybe, but an ogre would be bouncing his head against the roof, much less a giant."

The young man held up his hands in surrender. "I only know what the stories said, and even then, I didn't pay much attention to them. I thought they were just children's tales."

The Reeve boy swallowed heavily, then looked at the ruins. "We all did."

The Bad Badgers and their assorted hangers-on stared spellbound, as they'd been in the presence of the demon haunting the upper tunnels. With an effort of will, their leader cleared his throat and gave his head a shake to toss out the thought-blasting scale of the place and set his mind toward the next task.

"Well, elf," Torbjorn called, forcing himself to tear his eyes from the dreadful spectacle. "Since it is important that you be asked, is there anything you can tell us about this?"

For a second, the commander could have sworn he saw the svartalf's eyes dart toward the lass hunkered against Haeda, but it was so quick that he could have imagined it in the wavering light of the lanterns.

"Nothing comes to mind," the myrkling replied, then nodded forward. "But I believe we are coming to the end of this little tour. I can see a platform adjoining a structure and what looks like it might be a slope leading up."

A sigh of relief rippled through the cart, punctuated by a defiantly loud exclamation from Gromic.

"Erduna's dugs, that's good news."

"Quick, let's get that crank turning," Torbjorn barked without his usual volume. The place they stood seemed to demand quiet, and he only had so much will to marshal in defiance.

The cart had rolled to a stop on a platform below the upward slope. The wheels gave a dull *clank* as they settled into toothed sprockets set into the stone. A few strides from where the cart had come to rest was a crank for the winch, four stout bars jutting from a barrel-thick column of stone. At Torbjorn's command, Gromic, Waelon, Ober, and Tomza sprang from the cart and moved to the crank.

Haeda remained in the cart, one hand still resting on the girl, but she'd unshouldered her duabuw and braced the stock on her broad hip and was looking about with suspicious eyes. There was something foul in the air, and she wasn't the only one who felt it.

The commander of the crew hopped out of the cart and was joined by Utyrvaul. They moved away from the crank to squint at the structure set into the cavern wall overlooking the winch platform. At first, Torbjorn was comforted to see that the gantries and galleried alcoves were of dwarvish construction rather than the unhallowed architecture that dominated the cavern, but then he saw the bones. The unmistakably sturdy bones of dwarfs were scattered everywhere, desiccated scraps of flesh hanging in tatters to complete the grisly evidence of violence. Still worse were the scorched and defaced remains of the warding carvings scrawled across the structure.

"They came down here when the wights came," the commander mused, bile rising in his throat. "Trusting their wards would keep Ol' Whitey at bay while they waited for the enemy to pass."

The svartalf stood beside the dwarf, his flippant tone absent as he nodded.

"But the *mallevoug* was persistent and thought a little pain was worth the reward." Utyrvaul sighed. "It is a shame and a tragedy, not just for evil death they faced, but also because knowledge they gained from their efforts died with them."

Torbjorn's thumb ran across his scarred cheek. The platform gave a soft groan, then began to slowly rise from the efforts of the four dwarfs at the crank. He turned from the moldering tragedy to look across the waters at the ancient ruins.

"Perhaps that's for the best," he muttered, hoping to never see the sea giants' city or its like again. "Sometimes it's better for the past to keep its secrets and let Erduna swallow them. Some things are better left dead and buried."

"And some things will refuse to stay buried," the svartalf mused as they rose. "They are too patient and persistent for something as fleeting as death."

CHAPTER TWENTY-ONE

"Getting close."

The declaration was met by a chorus of dwarvish grunts. They'd been taking turns at the crank for hours, trudging in circles with heads bowed to keep the platform grinding upward. Typically, this sort of thing would be for beasts of burden or larger teams of workers, but the Bad Badgers had to make do with what they had. At least the unnerving disquiet had evaporated after they'd left the sunken city. It had been replaced by a fleeting hopefulness that sank into a weary doggedness as time crawled on and sweat dripped from noses and ran into beards.

"I feel bad that we can't help," Mabon admitted to Utyrvaul as they stood beside the cart, watching the crank turn steadily. "I would, but the handles are too low, and—"

"Shhh. It is all right, my little midge." The svartalf looked at the young man pityingly. "You'll soon learn that their kind love this sort of thing, and even more so when it gives them an opportunity to speak disparagingly of others. I'm willing to wager it will be a fortnight before we hear an end to their affectionate bellyaching over this incident."

Waelon raised his head and scowled at the pair.

"What was that, you blade-eared bastard?" he snarled as his shoulders shuddered and twitched. "You got something to say?"

"Just how very much I appreciate your efforts, darling," the elf called back with cheer. "Truly an inspiring display of fortitude both mental and physical. Really, I am awe-struck, and when we are out of these foul tunnels, I will compose a ballad inspired by your efforts."

The former ranger hawked and spat as he trod around the shaft of the crank, but the vengeful gobbet fell woefully short.

"I'd take a day's peace without you yammering over all the songs you could ever warble," he growled as he passed, his head drooping again as he marched on. "Damned lazy freeloading myrkling."

"You're a source of constant comedy, sweetie." Utyrvaul chortled and gave Mabon a sly sidelong look. "What did I tell you?"

Mabon's shoulders bobbed in a laugh, then a frown creased his smooth features.

"I don't think you should antagonize them," the Reeve lad opined. "They are doing all the work right now, and besides, I'm not sure how far you can push them."

"Oh, midge, take your pleasure where you can," the elf declared with a patronizing wag of his head. "If you're going to be traveling with our squat, sour friends, you're going to have to find ways to pass the time. Dwarf-baiting is one of my few consistently amusing diversions."

The young man looked away, his expression darkening as he glanced up. The lantern light had just touched the lip where the slope leveled.

"I'm not so sure," he muttered, the words low and hard.

"Not certain about dwarf-baiting or about remaining with our less-than-illustrious company?" Utyrvaul asked softly, leaning down to Mabon's shoulder. "Thinking of trying to give them the slip and making your way home, eh?"

The human recoiled from the elf but could only retreat so far before his heel bumped into the cart.

"No," he protested, his eyes darting toward the dwarfs. "You heard Torbjorn. If I go home now, everyone will know I helped you. They'll hang me as a traitor, and maybe the rest of my family."

The svartalf's red eyes flashed as he studied the young man's face, and Mabon felt naked before the shrewd look.

"Perhaps," he purred, slowly straightening, a knowing smile dancing about his thin face. "Though I'm certain a clever boy like you knows that things are rarely as set in stone as a dwarf might believe. A silver tongue and a dwarvish head in hand might go a long way to prove you are no traitor but a plucky hero who escaped a fate worse than death. Doesn't that sound like quite the tale?"

Mabon's eyes darted once more to the dwarfs, and again they seemed too busy laboring or recovering from their labors to pay the longshanks much attention. He'd only just let out the breath he'd been holding when he heard a scuff behind him in the cart and whirled to see the golden-eyed child staring at him. His heart jumped into his throat when he realized the girl had heard every word.

"I-I-I didn't say anything about k-killing anyone," he stammered as he held up open hands. "It was him. It was the elf! He—"

"Calm down, midge," Utyrvaul drawled, rolling his eyes. "This little treat hasn't said a word since we first found her, and your escape plans are unlikely to breach her vow of silence. Not after all the other things she's heard, isn't that right, my dear?"

The elf's long fingers reached toward the child, but she sprang back like a cat spying a viper that had snuck uncomfortably close. The only thing that arrested her retreat was the far side of the cart. Watching her little chest heaving in obvious fear, Mabon wasn't sure she wouldn't skitter out of the cart if the svartalf pressed her.

"I don't think she likes you," the young man observed. His stomach twisted when he saw the terror in the child's glinting eyes. "I'm not sure anyone here does."

"A fair observation," the myrkling remarked, studying the little one a heartbeat longer before turning back to Mabon. He grinned. "Which really is a shame since I adore every one of you."

The platform gave a lurch, then mechanisms ground and slid before there was a definitive *thunk*. The dwarfs around the crank heaved a collective groan of relief as they stepped away to gather their war gear.

"Right," Torbjorn rumbled, looking about after a long draw on a slack waterskin. "I think we're on foot again. This stonework here looks dwarvish again, and we've got to be within a dozen feet of the surface if not less. Seems we've got a better than good chance of finding another outlet, though whether it's a shaft or another secret basement, we'll see."

"Think we could have a minute, sir?" Gromic moaned as he leaned on his shield. "I imagine we're going to move quick-like once we hit sky, and I'm a touch worn."

The dwarf commander frowned as he looked around.

To be fair, Gromic and Waelon had taken the fewest breaks, insisting that the others, especially the freshly awoken Ober, needed to conserve their strength. Torbjorn had thrown himself into the task with them, but at one point, he'd realized he wasn't going to be worth much as a leader if he was too tired to think straight, so with pangs of guilt, he'd taken advantage of the extra rest when it was offered.

Now it looked as though he'd overestimated the seemingly inexhaustible reserves of the most powerful dwans. Gromic was still bracing his considerable bulk against his shield. Waelon was upright, but as Torbjorn watched him, the former ranger stared into space, teetering back and forth. He didn't know what awaited them above, though he hoped it was no more than a half-day's march to the Pickets. Regardless, they weren't going to be fit for much if he didn't give them a chance to rest.

"Good call, fordwan," Torbjorn nodded. "Breakout some food and catch your breath. We'll take a half-hour, then move on. The longshanks are on watch."

Gromic gave a grateful salute before collapsing on the spot, while Waelon managed a slightly more dignified slump against the tunnel wall. The other dwarfs had enough energy to draw some vittles out of their packs before settling to the floor. Seeing them sink to the stone, Torbjorn felt a tickle of unease at the back of his mind. Rather than join them, he snatched up a lantern and moved around the perimeter of their ad hoc camp.

He found that the rails went forward before turning a corner while the passage branched off. As he trod this northeasterly branch, the commander's dwarvish attunement to the earth told him the pitch of the floor went up.

"Stones and Bones," he whispered. "Let that be the way out."

"I supposed that optimistic declaration was more wishful thinking than certainty," Utyrvaul said, materializing out of the gloom behind him. "Ah, such are the burdens of leadership."

The dwarf, who'd nearly jumped out of his skin, spun, beard bristling and teeth bared.

"One of these days, elf," Torbjorn croaked, one hand on the hilt of his magsax. "One day, you're going to go in for a bit of fey foolery and find yourself with steel betwixt yer cheeks."

Utyrvaul's face twisted into a bemused smile, which was dispelled by a shake of the head to dismiss the image.

"That was poetry, commander," the svartalf said as he came over to stand with the dwarf. "But I'm afraid we have more pressing concerns."

Torbjorn tried to keep from heaving an immense sigh and settled for a draw through flaring nostrils as he ground his teeth.

"I saw you talking to our new friend," the commander stated, tilting his head toward the camp. "Is he planning something nefarious?"

Torbjorn knew it was a possibility, but he'd hoped otherwise. It wasn't that the human had no reason to hate him since the humiliation the lad had been through would have been enough. However, the commander had hoped the protection and potential benefits would outweigh his animosity. Still, if creatures could be counted on to choose grander cooperation over petty conflicts, the world would be a much different place.

"Disappointingly, no," the myrkling remarked, frowning. "Despite my best attempts, I'm afraid the midge is not fertile soil for the seeds of treachery to germinate and bloom."

Torbjorn scowled at the elf, fingers drumming on the pommel of his sword.

"Why would you try to get him to betray us?"

"Isn't it obvious?" Utyrvaul quipped, raising an incredulous eyebrow. "The longer the lad is with you lot, trusty and stalwart as you all are, the less likely that he is going to turn. Also, the more likely your guard is to be lowered. So, if the boy is going to betray us, it might as well be before he can do us much harm."

Torbjorn supposed that made twisted sense, though duplicity was as natural to him as daylight to a bat. He was aware it existed, but he'd endeavored to avoid it because it could be dangerous and downright painful. It wasn't that he'd never lied or schemed, but he'd given his word to the lad and his mother, and even disgraced as he was, that meant something to him.

"What would have happened if he'd taken to your suggestion?" Torbjorn asked.

"That, my friend, is a discussion for another time," the elf replied with one of his more unctuous smiles. "The key is that he did not, and that is not what I came here to talk to you about."

Were the myrkling closer to the ground, Torbjorn might have thumped him on the side of the head for the evasion. As it was, he ground his teeth a little more before raising a hand to his throbbing head.

"Fine," he growled from under the hand kneading at his temples. "What do you want to talk about?"

"We escaped the demon handily," the svartalf began, ignoring Torbjorn's scowl at the characterization of events. "But from the evidence we found by the winched platform, the fiend doesn't restrict itself to the upper layers. If it would travel miles deep for a bit of dwarvish flesh, why should we assume it would so easily give up the chase?"

Torbjorn ran a thumb over his fire-scored cheek, seeing the elf's point. He turned a suspicious eye to the darkness beyond the lanterns' light.

"Maybe it decided we weren't worth the effort," he offered, though his words didn't strike even him as convincing. "Maybe it can't die from mortal weapons, but a few bolts and a hatchet to the head left it in a bad way for some time. Maybe it fears we'll do that again before we find a way to actually hurt it."

Utyrvaul shook his head to dismiss the suggestion out of hand. "I'm afraid you are applying a far too rational mindset to that being. That would make sense if this were a simple predator, a creature of flesh and blood for whom consumption was an equation of resources gained checked by resources expended, or if it feared us. If it thought we were a real threat, it wouldn't have toyed with Ober and his…passenger. No, I'm fairly certain this is part of the game it is playing."

Torbjorn didn't like the idea, but he had to admit there was sense to it. He understood these matters even worse than he did matters of snake-tongued duplicity.

"To what end?" the dwarf asked, fingers settling on the magsax's hilt again.

"I carried on a dalliance with a sorceress," the myrkling began, throwing out a quick wink. "She insisted that *mallevoug*, being entities of metaphysical consumption, *tasted* the emotional resonance of the creatures they consumed. It stands to reason that a fiend like that might view this not as hunting but rather as a form of cooking."

Torbjorn's sword came free as an angry rumbled formed in his chest.

"So, it lets us run and feel something like hope," he growled, grinding out the words. "All to season us to its taste."

"Precisely," the elf replied, his blade in hand. "I think we ought to try leaping out of this frying pan to see if the fire suits us any better."

"You think it's watching, already sensing a change in the recipe?" the dwarf commander asked.

"We can't afford to assume otherwise," Utyrvaul replied, his body poised while his piercing eyes scanned the darkness.

Torbjorn nodded and drew a huge breath to fill his broad chest.

"Bad Badgers!" he bellowed with enough force that all but the svartalf jumped. "Stow and go time! Come on, move yourselves! Shield bearers to the front!"

Their commander's tone drove any thought of complaint from the weary dwarfs. They sprang up and started cramming their kits together. Gromic and Waelon, neither of whom had managed to get around to a hasty bite, rose with slumped shoulders and red-rimmed eyes, but their shields were in front of them, inscribed boards shining.

"Come on, girl," Haeda called, bending for the lass to mount her back. The dwarfess could sense they were in for a long, hard slog and intended to spare herself and the child the effort of attempting the mount-up in mid-flight.

The girl moved forward to comply, but as she clambered up, her gaze rose, and she lurched backward. Haeda, feeling the application and rapid evacuation of weight on her back, swung around with a frustrated question on her lips. Then she saw the child's pointing finger and terrified expression.

The dwarfess made to draw her magsax, but a gnarled fist flattened her to the stones. Breath wooshed from the driver's body before stars burst inside her head as it rebounded off the floor with the force of the blow. Voiceless and stunned, her body writhed as one part fought for air while the other was still trying to free her sword.

The sound of the heavy blow, along with Haeda's mail scraping across the stones, attracted the eyes of her companions, and they cried out in revulsion and anger. The monster's body twisted to crab across the ceiling like a maggot-ridden spider, grinning at the rest of the crew as it hung over the stricken dwarfess. The clotted eyes twinkled beneath their filmy rime, and a laugh as jagged and thin as a blade of glass sawed across every ear.

So close, teased the reedy, grating presence in their minds. *So, so close.*

Shouting a fear-sharpened battle cry, Ober rushed forward, magsax drawn and ready to thrust upward. The demon continued to laugh, the sound threatening to fill and drown every mind as it detached from the tunnel's roof to meet the charging dwarf.

"Your shield, lad!" Torbjorn shouted, but too late. Ober flew forward and drove the magsax into the open hand of the fiend. Crooked fingers closed around the weapon as dirty yellow effluence ran over the hilt and the hand holding it, then the young dwarf was forced to release his weapon to keep from having his arm torn off.

Bolts from Tomza's and Torbjorn's duabuws thudded into the wormy flesh. They were mere nuisances, prompting the barest snarl from the demon as it batted Ober aside with a contemptuous swat. The young dwan twisted away from the blow, but the creature's strength sent him rolling across the floor to fetch up against the far wall.

Dessssssert, came the mental whisper, lascivious as it dragged over their minds.

Torbjorn had scooped up Ober's forgotten shield and joined ranks with Gromic and Waelon as they rushed toward Ol' Whitey, but the fiend was already springing toward Tomza. She dropped her duabuw and reached for her shield, but the demon seized her throat. She abandoned the shield in a desperate attempt to keep her head from being popped off, although her fingers clawed at the hand. Slack skin rent and tore but the grip remained adamant.

Then Tomza sailed through the air, and her armored body smashed into the three dwarfs rushing forward. To keep from being struck by the dwarfess' flying form, Gromic, Waelon, and Torbjorn broke ranks and were rewarded by being flattened into a tangle of limbs and shields.

"Well, this isn't how I planned to die," Utyrvaul hissed as he sprang over the toppled dwarfs, sword to the fore. "Come on, midge. Let's get this over with."

Mabon drew his father's blade in a sweaty hand and moved to follow, but he was neither as long-legged nor as agile as the elf and was forced to scramble around the pile of dwarfs that blocked the tunnel.

Spriteling, Ol' Whitey tittered as it bore Utyrvaul's slashing strokes with bored indifference. *Some time since I tasted spriteling*.

Despite an impressive display of martial prowess, all it took was a surge forward, ignoring the blade tip ramming into its pendulous belly, to plant a kick in the elf's stomach that sent him tumbling backward. The young human had cleared the dwarfs and had to throw himself flat to avoid the elf hurtling past him. Before he could rise, a knob-knuckled rap on the skull flattened him on the stones.

Fun, fun, fun, crowed the demon as it wheeled, reveling in its dominion. As it capered, its gaze fell upon the girl cowering beside the dwarfess, who was fighting to rise.

Something new, something old, it wheezed as it stalked forward. *What, oh, what will this taste like?*

Rubbing twisted fingers together, it pranced the last few steps before reaching down with a hand to snatch the child up. Torbjorn shouted as he rose from one knee, and Haeda, her gaze still unfocused, tried to get in front of the child, only to fall to her hands and knees. Black fangs ran with translucent saliva in anticipation.

Wonder, wonder, wonder.

Then the girl looked up, her golden eyes blazing with the light of a sun's last glory. Ol' Whitey's approaching digits faltered and withdrew smoking, beaten back by the violent brilliance pouring from those eyes. In a place that had not known such light for epochs, an angry star dawned, and its furious revelation was unstoppable and merciless. The demon recoiled, scrambling back on jellied legs as the child strode forward, a silhouette in which burned a presence of frightening potency.

Mercy, mercy, mercy, the fiend wailed as it prostrated itself in supplication. *We serve, we serve, we serve. I serve she of the Gates.*

The child looked down at the thing coiling in the dust at her feet. Her lips curled in disgust below her searing gaze, then parted, and from that mouth came the cataclysmic chorus of an inferno, each leaping tongue rolling to form the voice of an angry god.

"VERMIN BUZZING ABOVE THE KING'S TABLE," declared the presence within and behind the child. "FAITHLESS PARASITE CLINGING TO BROKEN OATHS. FAILED FINAL GUARDIAN, BANISHED AND ABJURED."

No!

The piteous ephemeral wail cut across the souls of all who looked on like a razor, but the terrible light flared. Mortal and elvish hands rose to shield eyes and faces, but the light shone through flesh like paper, inescapable.

RETURN! RETURN, SUNKEN AND EMPTY, TO WHET THE APPETITES OF YOUR MASTERS!

NO!

The demon fought to its wobbling legs, whether to attack or flee would never be known. The presence suffusing the girl spoke a single syllable that set the air alight and filled its mind with immolating thoughts. Under this onslaught, the demon dubbed Ol' Whitey kindled like cloth, flaring with unclean light before its body came apart in a puff of ash. Floating amid that ash seethed a dark presence that was invisible yet undeniable. In some other place, it hung between worlds, tormented and shattered before it too fled the light.

With that ultimate retreat, the light vanished from the child as quickly as a candle was snuffed out. The girl sank to the ground, curling into a fetal ball in her patchwork coat.

After the dazzling light faded, all were left blinking and blind, their watering eyes scrambling to adjust in the sudden gloom. The lantern light, now woefully inadequate, showed wet faces staring about like noon-woken owls. Shuddering breaths were taken, mouths opening only to close again as minds reeled.

There came a rumble from deep in the earth, then the sharp crack of stone breaking.

"What's happening?" Ober cried as he staggered over to Haeda and helped her regain her feet, holding on as she swayed.

"Final guardian," Gromic muttered as he hauled Tomza up. "That's what she called it."

"Last thing keeping this place together." Torbjorn grunted as he stepped cautiously toward the child. "Which was why they never tried to drive it out."

"Who?" Waelon asked, trudging over to scoop up Mabon, who was still lying senseless on the ground.

"The heretic dwarfs, of course." Utyrvaul groaned as he climbed to his feet without his typical grace. "Let's get moving before we get trapped down here with them."

"The girl," Haeda cried, tearing herself free from the young dwarf's grip to change direction.

Torbjorn stood over the child, or what they'd wanted to believe was a child, feeling the tunnel vibrate beneath his boots.

"Tweldwan?" Gromic called, his voice quavering.

Shaking his shaggy head and calling himself a fool, the commander bent and scooped up the girl. Her eyes fluttered, but the terrifying light wasn't there—only the peculiar golden color, now plain in comparison.

"Get moving!" Torbjorn shouted as he turned, the child cradled to his chest. "We didn't come this far to be buried alive."

CHAPTER TWENTY-TWO

"I never thought I'd be so happy to see the Cloud Sea."

Waelon's confession was lost amid the grinding crash of the building behind them as they moved clear of the pluming dust. The Bad Badgers had raced down the tunnel and emerged in the bowels of a fire-gutted homestead. Decades-old fires and the entropic touch of the surface elements had left a structure that seemed as structurally sound as an eggshell, but the stairs to the ground floor, like most things in a dwarvish home, were stone. The crew had scrambled up the crumbling stones with dust and the ghost of evil memories blasting from the tunnel mouth behind them. It was tricky to move across the few splintering beams to solid ground, but they managed, and they stood panting as they stared around.

It seemed they'd never left the glade around the Reeve home since there was a frost-rimed forest around them. A slumped, buckling woodshed stood near the house, and a barn...well, calling it a barn would have been dishonest, but it had once been a barn. The longer they stood there gazing about, the more it seemed to be an oracular vision of what the Reeve home would look like when it went the way of all mortal things. After the unnatural preservation in the deeps below, it might have provided some assurance of the natural order, but it was sullied by the aura of the place.

The trees pressed closer, the timbered sentinels of the woods suspicious of sending their offspring toward the desolate homestead. Even the ground around the place, which was coated in dust and ice, was darkened and dry, as though the fire that had gnawed the heart out of the buildings was only days old rather than years. The wearing and weathering had happened, but the greening and growing had not. It was a place mindlessly merciless plants pressed each other toward even as they twisted away and where no bird or beast would shelter even if hunter and hounds were hot on their trail.

A blighted and broken place on the doorstep of a fiend's domicile.

"Let's keep moving," Torbjorn instructed, adjusting the girl in his arms so he could draw his cloak out of his pack and drape it over both of them. After the display in the dark, he doubted the girl was in any danger of getting cold, but when he looked at her, he saw a child, and he had little choice in the matter.

Children—dwarf, elf, human, whatever else—were meant to be protected and shielded, and nothing would convince the commander otherwise.

Cradling the softly snoring bundle in his arms, Torbjorn led their ragged group northward. Sick with the horror of the place they'd left and hollow from the dread of what they'd seen with the demon's banishment, none spoke as they trudged on. They leaned on one another, expressions slack as one foot was mechanically placed in front of the other. As they left the soiled presence of the dead homestead behind, their eyes fixed on the earth just ahead of their next step. The bleak beauty of the alpine valley surrendering to the deathly season was lost on them.

Even when the trees parted to reveal the projecting crown of their destination, it seemed that none had noticed. There was no cheer to see one of the Southern Pickets stabbing heavenward, or any commentary at all. They just trudged on, boots crunching the cold-stiffened underbrush with each step.

None of them seemed to notice when hunched, low-slung shapes darted between the trees around them. Even Utyrvaul's face was downcast, and his breath was a weary rasp in his ears, so he was blind to the forms encircling them.

To his credit, Torbjorn sensed something was off and paused to raise his head and look about. The wind whistled through the treetops, and he was sure something was watching them, but his weary eyes still could not pick out the dark, lumpy shapes clinging to the cover of the trees.

"Hold," he called over his shoulder and heard the stammering scuff of boots coming to a halt behind him. In the back of his mind, the sound told him how spread out they were, too broken in spirit and endurance to keep a cohesive formation. They were done fighting for the day, and whoever was watching had to know it. That or they were stupid.

"I know you're out there," he shouted, his voice hoarse and weak. "Just come out, and let's get this over with."

For a heartbeat, there was nothing. Torbjorn looked over his shoulder and saw his bedraggled forces. They had a bolt or two between them, and were bruised, bloodied, and barely able to keep their feet. Whoever had come to prey on them had selected the perfect time. At this point, they'd be lucky to get their swords out and their shields raised before they caught an arrow in the throat.

As though reading his thoughts, there was the whirring *thwack* of a duabuw, and the hard earth a half-step in front of Torbjorn fetched up around a quivering bolt. He didn't have the energy or inclination to jump at the display, but he squinted at the familiar projectile.

"Don't move!" came a gruff dwarvish voice from the trees.

"We've got you surrounded! One wrong move, and you'll be pincushions!"

Torbjorn nodded and cocked his head over his shoulder.

"As I'm sure you've noticed," he began with a heavy sigh, "none of us are in any shape to argue. Point of fact, the most danger you're in would be shooting at a dwan ready to collapse, seein' as you've got us surrounded. You're as likely to shoot at each other as us when we flop down on the earth."

For a time, there was no answer from the timber, and Torbjorn frowned. It had made sense in his fatigue-addled mind, but now he was uncertain whether what he'd meant had translated.

There were low whispers between the trunks, and Torbjorn thought he saw crouched shapes amid the undergrowth.

"Would you like us to—"

"Shut up!" the gruff voice shouted, and Torbjorn could almost hear fingers curling around taut triggers. "Claim your allegiance and explain why you're sneaking around a dwarvish military fortification."

Torbjorn frowned and considered pointing out that he couldn't do the latter if he obeyed the former, but the ambush leader's voice warned him that he was in no mood to be trifled with. There was a raw tension there that Torbjorn wouldn't have expected from a commander operating along the contested border, especially when it came to apprehending broken stragglers. Something else was afoot.

"We serve in the Sufstan Holt'Dwan at the direction of Lardwan Klaus of Gevin," Torbjorn declared, squaring his shoulders. "We've been on an operation and are now tasked with returning to the holt'dwan with our objective."

There was more whispering before the ambush leader spoke again.

"Sufstan's already at Grayshelf," the gruff voice announced, suspicion lacing the words. "You lads are a good ways behind your holt'dwan if that's where you're really from, though you look more like vagabonds in stolen armor."

Fatigue stoked the irritation that drove heat into Torbjorn's reply.

"What part of "operation" slipped past your keen ears, Fordwan? If we were bound for wight territory, wouldn't it stand to reason that we'd be a fair bit behind the army? And wouldn't you also imagine that trudging through enemy territory to the Pickets is why we're so damned rundown?"

There was another heavy silence followed by more rasping susurrations while the wind overhead released trickles of snow that passed between branches.

"You're not rangers, and we've been told to expect no patrols." The voice was a touch uncertain. "What's to say you aren't deserters or traitors come to spy for the wheezers?"

Ah, there it was.

The wight lord's movement at Paelon's Watch had been noted, and people were getting nervous along the line of fortifications. With the nearest holt'dwan leagues northward, they were vulnerable, and a large enemy force had appeared over the mountains. It was every fear confirmed, and fear made even level-headed dwarfs suspicious and stupid.

"I'm not sure how I'm going to convince a bunch of trees of my allegiance," Torbjorn called, hoping he sounded amused rather than scornful. "But if I could look a dwan in the eye, a fordwan could make up his mind before we all freeze to death."

The silence was shorter this time, and the serpentine conversation was also brief.

"Throw down your arms. We'll search you, then we'll see about that conversation."

Torbjorn didn't like the solution, but he'd expected it, and if the tables were turned, he'd have done the same thing.

"You heard him, dwans," Torbjorn called over his shoulder. "Everything on the ground. I'm not going to speak for the fordwan, but I'm willing to bet that if he finds so much as a sharp spoon, he'll be in a foul temper, so nothin' clever, you hear?"

His people grunted and muttered, but shortly after that, he heard the clangs and clatters of weapons meeting frost-stiffened earth. Torbjorn let his duabuw tumble free, then his shield. He shuffled the girl from arm to arm to tug out his sword and dagger. The child's eyes fluttered, and she gave a sniff as she was shifted to draw the cloak about her shoulders.

By the time Torbjorn looked up from his efforts, a ring of armed dwarfs had sprung up around them, advancing with crossbows held at their shoulders. Directly in front of Torbjorn was a hard-eyed dwarf with heavy scar tissue wound through his dirty blond beard, his eyes fixed on the bundle in the leader's arms.

"What's that?" the dwarf asked. It was the fordwan Torbjorn had been conversing with. "Throw it down like the rest."

"Why?" the ambush leader demanded. "What do you think it is?"

"Look," the commander of the Bad Badgers instructed, and he slowly moved aside his cloak to reveal the girl's face. Snowflakes settled on dark lashes and a smooth cheek, and the child curled inward for warmth again.

"That's no dwarf," the fordwan stated accusingly, though his pale eyes seemed more confused than angry. Then he saw Mabon and Utyrvaul. "What are you doing toting around some long-shanks bairn, along with another human and a myrkling?"

Torbjorn tucked the girl in, then turned a flat expression to the fordwan.

"That's something to ask Lardwan Klaus."

The hard eyes narrowed, and for half a heartbeat, Torbjorn was sure he was one word from a bolt in the eye, so he just waited.

"You'll carry her under guard, but the rest of your command will be bound," the ranger fordwan growled as though cutting off an argument. "Check 'em over, then lash 'em up, lads. The tweldwan will sort 'em out."

"Fordwan," Torbjorn began but paused to soften his tone when he saw the cutting look from the scarred dwarf. "We're under orders by the lardwan of the Sufstan Holt'Dwan to report to him as soon as possible. You're keeping us from doing our duty if you drag us to the Pickets to sit in the cells—"

"You think I should just let you hop on by?" the fordwan interrupted with a sneer. "Just take you at your word?"

Torbjorn fought to keep his tone even as he noticed rangers creeping closer.

"If you haven't noticed, we're not hopping anywhere. Going to the Pickets was part of our plan to catch our breath and resupply before heading to Grayshelf. I'm just asking you not to—"

"What I'm hearing is this," the sour dwarf interjected, an ugly smile twisting the scars on his face. "That's something to ask Tweldwan Jozef from behind a set of iron bars."

Before the leader of the Bad Badgers could respond, the fordwan turned to his dwarfs and raised his voice.

"Turn 'em inside out, and if they resist or are hiding anything, put a bolt through their skulls."

CHAPTER TWENTY-THREE

"Really, you're making this harder than it needs to be."

Torbjorn had given the same answer he'd given several times, but they'd shoved a gag into his mouth to keep him accidentally biting through his tongue as their fists smashed into him. They couldn't have him choking on his blood and lisping indistinguishably when they finally broke him, could they? That would render all this extra effort rather pointless.

Torbjorn supposed he should have appreciated the thoughtfulness in sparing his teeth and tongue, but it was hard to appreciate anything as another heavy blow smashed into his belly.

"Let's try this again." Tweldwan Jozef of Merihn sighed and ran his thick fingers over the gray-streaked braids in his beard. "What did the lardwan send you out to do?"

Rough hands seized Torbjorn, their owners' breath of hot in his face as one forced his head back and the other roughly tore the gag from his mouth. A small, angry voice told the dwarf commander to snap at the hand, hoping to snare a finger to tear and grind at, but the louder yet wearier voices won. Biting off a finger of tweldwan's bully boys wasn't going to help.

But to that point, neither was anything else Torbjorn could do.

"I was sworn to secrecy by the lardwan." He coughed, tasting the blood coating the back of his throat. "My dwans don't know anything, and the others are just strays we picked up along the way. If you want answers, send for the lardwan, or better yet, take us—"

Torbjorn's weary explanation was silenced when, at a nod from Jozef, the two brutish dwans grabbed him and shoved the gag back into place. This time the spiteful voice won, and he managed to scrape a furrow in some knuckles before the dwarf they belonged to pulled his hand away. Torbjorn was rewarded with several sharp blows to the face. At least one of them knocked his nose off-kilter with a wet snap before he tumbled back in the chair he was bound to.

"All right, all right. That's enough," the tweldwan called as boots began to stomp down. "Stones, if he's dead, he can't tell us a thing! Get off him, you idiots. Get off and go!"

The battering ceased, and through watering eyes, Torbjorn saw Jozef kneel next to his head.

"How about you let me tell you something," whispered the dwarvish officer and castellan of the eastern line of Pickets. "I know you are shabr'dwan, and I don't begrudge you for not sharing that since it certainly wouldn't have warmed your reception, but let me help you understand how we're both in a situation to recover this mess."

As he spoke, the tweldwan reached down and picked at bloodied strands of Torbjorn's hair that had fallen in front of his face. It seemed the castellan believed Torbjorn would understand if his view were unimpeded.

"It might not seem like it, but we're in similar positions."

Despite the pain, Torbjorn had the wherewithal to give the tweldwan an incredulous scowl.

"I know it sounds hard to believe, but it's true," Jozef insisted in a conspiratorial tone. "We've both been abandoned by our superiors and are facing an impossible situation. You see, there is a wheezer assault force heading toward my little corner of the Pickets. You and I both know these fortifications were made to fend off raiders and give early warning to the nearest holt'dwan. A force of the size that's come over the mountain is beyond our ability to resist. That means the best we can hope to do is slow them as they bring these walls down on our heads while your holt'dwan sits snug up in Grayshelf all winter."

Torbjorn was having a hard time thinking clearly, but all things considered, he was following the tweldwan's logic. If the wight lord had brought the kind of force they'd seen at the Teeth, the Pickets would be lucky to slow them down. Jozef nodded fervently at his prisoner as though willing him to stay with that train of thought.

"Now, I can't very well abandon the Pickets with as many dwans as I can gather, not without ending up...well, ending up in a circumstance you're probably familiar with. No offense to you and your past indiscretions, but I haven't climbed this high just to see myself scraping away at the Deeping or as fodder for some spymaster. No, I'll face a wheezer before that happens, but there's no reason for it to happen if I have a reason to retreat—some vital piece of information that needs protecting and escorting to those bastards squatting in Grayshelf."

Torbjorn had suspected this was what it was about, but he'd wanted to believe it was otherwise. He winced as a weary sigh tried to whistle through his broken nose and settled for contemplating the cell floor. Looking at the officer made him sick.

He didn't know why it stung him so deeply to see it up close, but it did—every time.

"All right, all right," Jozef snapped, a desperate edge sharpening his irritation at the wordless rejection. "You're holding on to some vainglorious idea that is going to get hundreds of dwans killed needlessly, but think about this. My rangers found that little map you had tucked away, and we know you came from the Teeth on the other side of the mountain's arm."

Torbjorn refused to look up at the tweldwan, but he knew where this was going too. This certainty was accompanied not by a nauseous disgust but rising anger he couldn't keep out of his eyes.

"That's right," the castellan hissed, one hand holding back his braids as he leaned within inches of Torbjorn's ear. "I know why they're here! They're following you. I don't know if it's the elf, the lad, the lass, or something else, but that wheezer isn't charging across the Vale with winter setting in for nothing. We both know they're too smart for that, but we also know that wights are relentless, and if you've got something they want, they're not going to worry about enemy fortifications or the damned cold. We also know that if the wheezer gets its bony claws on what it wants, it has no reason to be so reckless."

A low, rumbling growl began in Torbjorn's chest, and Josef started, nearly toppling onto his wide backside. The commander of the Bad Badgers glared at the tweldwan, a deep but ever-fresh hatred shining in his dark eyes.

"That's fine. Hate me, curse me, damn me with every oath you know," the officer spat, his teeth bared behind his mustache. "But know this. You'll either give me what I need to save my command and your motley lot, or I'll feed you all to the wheezer and hope for the best."

Torbjorn continued to stare, the force of the growl subsiding as the fire in his chest condensed to a single smoldering ember.

"I've drawn my patrols back, but by all accounts, you got here just ahead of the vanguard," the castellan explained, his eyes boring into his prisoner's. "You understand what that means, don't you? You're running out of time to decide."

His neck stiff from the abuse he'd received, Torbjorn nodded his understanding.

"Do you have anything to say while it still matters?"

Torbjorn nodded again. Careful to keep his hand as clear of the prisoner's hazardous teeth, Jozef dragged the gag out of his mouth.

"Well?"

"You're a coward, but know this," Torbjorn rasped into the tweldwan's face. "You're going to die here, probably screaming like a frightened pig. I just hope I'm around to see it."

CHAPTER TWENTY-FOUR

"You still alive in there, Tweldwan?"

Torbjorn had been unceremoniously deposited on the floor after being dragged out of the interrogation cell. At the moment, he wasn't certain how to answer Gromic's question. The castellan hadn't taken his declaration with much grace, and that, on top of the beating he'd already endured, had left him uncertain about his current state. Besides his nose, there was now something clicking in his neck that sent sheets of seizing fire down one side of his body, and he'd lost all feeling in his left hand, though that might have been from having his wrists bound to the chair.

Still, he knew his dwans were waiting for him, every second of his silence sapping their hearts.

"For the moment." He groaned, swallowing another mouthful of blood-clogged spittle. "How's everyone else? We all here?"

"A few bumps and bruises from mouthing off to those limp-wristed elf-suckers," Waelon growled from down the line of cells. "But yeah, we're all here, sir. Well, except for the girl."

"I can assure you not even a wosealf would let this brutish lot anywhere near their musky behind."

Torbjorn tried to sit up sharply, but his neck gave another click, and the right side of his body went into painful contractions. His body curled around the pained fit, and it was several seconds before he could force enough breath into his lungs to speak and several more before he had enough to be heard.

"Where...Erduna's arse...ugh, where did they take her?" he called as he did his best to unclench his contorted body.

"Stuck the poor thing in a grem-cage, the bastards," Haeda cried, and Torbjorn heard the stout bars of her cell rattle. "If they hurt that lass, I'll burn this whole kaking place to the ground with those kak-sacks inside."

"Someone might beat you to it," Torbjorn moaned as he scooted across the floor to rest his back against the icy stone walls. The cold rock was a boon to his throbbing, aching body, but he sucked in a breath as the touch prickled his flushed skin.

"What was that?" Gromic shouted.

"The wheezer's coming," Torbjorn declared loudly enough for all to hear. "The castellan is pretty sure they're coming for us, and he's saying that if I don't tell him what Klaus sent us out for and what we're bringing back to him, he's going to hand us over."

"How does telling him about the mission help him against the wights?" Tomza hollered from farther down the hall.

"It gives him an excuse to run away," Torbjorn answered, battling the urge to nod off as he lay against the wall. The last of the agonized tension unraveled under the frosty press of the wall. "If he withdraws to Grayshelf without having some secret information to protect, he'll rightly be called a coward, and you know the rest."

"I assume you took the obnoxiously noble route," Utyrvaul groused from a nearby cell. "Which means he'd rather stay here and take his chances with the wights by giving us up than withdraw from a fight he can't win and try to sort out the coward business while he's still alive?"

"More or less." Torbjorn grunted as he shifted to make himself more comfortable. "Though if he wasn't lying about the scouting reports, his options for retreat were negligible anyway. He said the vanguard was right behind the forces that brought us in, which means now they're prob—"

There was a succession of sounds, not a single noise but an ear-hammering cacophony from far beyond the stone walls that enclosed them. No single note or voice was discernible, but for the veterans among the crew, it was as familiar as the voice of a well-known creature.

The wight had come.

They heard the fortification take up arms, the rattles and clanks of armored dwarfs moving around each other while stores of arms were laid out and positions fortified. Deep voices bellowed and roared as officers of the line marshaled and directed their dwans to prepare to hold the Picket to the bitter end.

Torbjorn might have been heartened by the sounds if he hadn't known who was in command. He wasn't fool enough to think that all or even most of the soldiers preparing the defenses were good dwarfs. Most of them were like him, a jumble of ambition, pride, and folly, but he knew there would be some who were as good as the dwans he'd led to this bitter end. He had no tears for this realization, no sobs of remorse for his failures and mistakes. He'd done his best for what little that had amounted to, and it had led him here.

He might have regretted failing to lead them better or failing to *be* better, but doing so might have meant he would never have found himself here with them. He did *not* regret that.

It was unfortunate that the Bad Badgers had to wait for the end like this, cooped up in pens like beasts awaiting slaughter. However, they would return to their clans as dwans who'd fallen being true to the charge given them, and that…well, that had to count for something.

"Not the first time I've said this, though it will be the first time some of you have heard it," Torbjorn called to the cells holding his charges. "But I'm pleased to be serving with you, as always."

A stillness descended over their cell block as all around them, the Picket continued its raucous preparations.

"Even the myrkling?" Utyrvaul asked. Torbjorn could hear his sardonic smile.

Torbjorn grunted a curse under his breath while dragging himself to his feet, then wearily limped to the bars of his cell.

"Even him," Torbjorn intoned sincerely, adding his own wry smile. "Though that might be true only because I won't live to regret it."

Grim laughter, dark but honest, rose from every cell lining the hallway, except the one farthest from Torbjorn's, from which there came a strangled growl.

"What's that?" Waelon shouted, the bars ringing as he snatched at them to press himself to look down the hall. "What's going on?"

"It's Ober," Tomza called from the far cell, which adjoined her brother's. "There's something wrong. Ober, what's going on?"

They all waited with bated breath, and there was another choked growl from the farthest cell.

"Just trying...argh, to...to wake somebody...somebody up."

Dwarfs, elf, and Mabon pressed against the bars, straining to see what was happening.

"What is he talking about?" Gromic asked.

"Is something hurting him?" Haeda called.

"Sounds like he's hurting himself," Waelon added. "Oi, Ober! What are you doing?"

Tomza was the first to realize, and she raised her voice in an urgent scream.

"Everyone! Get away from the bars! Furthest corner, *now*!"

There was a babble of half-formed questions before the

dwarfs and elf realized what was about to happen and scrambled to obey.

Only the unlucky elder son of the Reeve family stood at his cell door, brow furrowed as he strained to see.

"I don't understand," he shouted, voice cracking in frustration and fear. "What's going o—"

The ursine roar that answered his question sent the young man scampering to the far corner of his cell.

As one would expect, the cells for captives of the Picket, not expansive enough to be a dungeon, were located in the lowest reaches of the fortification. At first, it seemed there was an earthquake occurring in the foundations of the tower. In the rattle and din of preparing for the enemy onslaught, the initial rumbles were barely noticed by any but the most perceptive. Even then, they were dismissed when the dwarfs saw the wight's forces marching out of the woods to fill the cleared land in front of the westward Pickets.

The rumbling became a roar that was joined by the crack of masonry shattering and the screams of frightened soldiers. Though there was danger without, and the fleeting shapes of gremalkins were visible in the moonlight, there was also danger within.

Out of the bowels of the fortress it came, roaring and snarling, its huge, hairy form buckling and cracking the walls of the corridors it barreled through. The dwans in the tower, a skeleton force guarding the prisoners, were the first to see it. They were the luckiest since they had no time for true terror. Their minds reeled at the sudden appearance of the behemoth that burst out of the cells and set upon them with fang and claw. All but one was killed before they had time to draw their weapons, and the single survivor didn't waste time scrabbling for the sword at his belt but opted to run. His decision bought him a minute more than his fellows before he too was thrown down and torn apart. His final scream awakened the rest of the tower to what was coming for them.

It didn't matter.

On the square curtain wall surrounding the Picket's base, the dwan garrison had begun loosing bolts at the skirmishing gremalkin that dared to come near. At rounded redoubts along that wall, torsion-powered launchers primed by two dwarfs and aimed by a third began launching clay vessels filled with an alchemical fire solution at the nearest ranks of undead. Those soldiers on the wall heard the chaos within the tower behind them, but they had more pressing matters.

Within the tower, things had gone from bad to ruinous very quickly. Some of those within attempted to concentrate their strength to face this unlooked-for monster rampaging through the fortress, yet wherever dwarfs moved to counterattack, there came a storm of blood and thunderous roars that left parts of them littering the stairs, floors, and furnishings. Their bolts were leaves thrown at a hurricane, and their blades bent and snapped like straw in a hailstorm. It was no mere creature of flesh and blood—it couldn't be—but a vengeful elemental force before which their weapons were laughably insufficient.

Others, at the direction of their frantic tweldwan, scrambled to deny the furious storm, throwing up obstacles in mounting desperation. These proved to be as woefully ineffective as the ill-fated attacks, the barricades smashed with contemptuous ease. Doorways, locked and barred, were battered through, the stout constructs torn from their mounts to come crashing down on any foolish enough to shelter behind them. One such doorway being blasted from its moorings ripped a sizable chunk of wall apart. Terrified dwarfs seized the opportunity to leap through the opening to the courtyard below. Several landed badly, limbs snapping under their armored bulk, while a few managed to roll with the bruising impact, coming up relatively whole.

It made little difference.

The ursine storm burst from the confines of the tower and hurtled down upon them like a meteor of dark fur.

The garrison on the wall saw what had raised such consternation behind them, eyes bulging within their helmets as the first ranks of the enemy assaulted the walls. In the courtyard below was a hellish mockery of a bear pulling apart armored dwarfs like sweetmeats, while before them, the first ranks of the undead clutched and clambered at the lips of the walls. Bellows to hold fast roared across the curtain wall, and to a dwarf, they obeyed if for no other reason than fleeing to the tower risked painting the cold cobbles with their steaming blood.

Over by the gatehouse, this distraction had proved less than fortuitous as a pack of lithe gremalkins led by a great chieftain of their kind sprang into action and leapt up the wall in two bounds. The dwarfs manning the gates while eyeing the monster in the courtyard by the light of their watchfires were caught unawares by other claws that snared and dragged them down before long fangs delivered the fatal bites. The chieftain dispatched his kin to unseat the stout iron-banded timber barring the gates while the others shed their skins to attend to the spoked wheels bound to the chains attached to the doors. With a low groan like a death knell, the gates of the Picket's curtain wall slowly began to slide open.

Across the killing field before the Picket, a pair of coldly gleaming eyes watched intently. Their owner, clad in his patina regalia for war and seated upon a huge skeletal destrier, had not expected so quick an opportunity, but his unliving will quickened to seize upon it. With a war cry as shrill as a banshee's wail, the wight lord raised his sword, which shone with a baleful light, and launched his steed forward. Keening after their master with unthinking, unwavering loyalty, the ranks of lifeless cavaliers spurred the fleshless flanks of their mounts.

So approached the lance of the wight lord like an arrow aimed at the heart of the dwarfs' tower, while within the storm of blood still raged.

CHAPTER TWENTY-FIVE

"Find the lass, and let's get out of here."

Torbjorn's instructions, after they'd all managed to bash and kick their way out of their mangled cells, were met with nods, then boots bounded over the trail of shattered stone the transformed Ober had left. Predictably, Haeda was at the head of the group, calling for the child as she raced upward.

The others followed her, but Tomza and Gromic hung back with their commander as he limped his way up.

"Steady on, Tweldwan. I've gotcha," the stout dwarf said, sliding under Torbjorn's arm and putting his arm around the battered leader's back. "Just you lean on me."

"Sir, what about my brother?" Tomza pressed as she shuffled a step behind the pair.

Torbjorn didn't have enough breath to respond since he was fighting the seizing muscles on his right side. A few more staggering steps, and even with Gromic's support, he was drawing hissing breaths between clenched teeth. By the time they reached the first steps, Gromic practically carrying him, he had to call for a break. His head and vision swam with the pain, while his body refused to answer his insistent calls that it relinquish control to him and cease this agonizing rebellion.

Pitched up against the cold stones, it was all he could do to draw one breath and let out the next.

"We're not going to get out of here in time," Gromic growled, raking his thick fingers through his beard. "Those bastards really did a number on him."

Tomza heard the roar of her spirit-haunted brother above them, and her chest tightened with anxiety. Then she turned to see the pain-pinched face of her commander, who lay broken at her feet.

One crisis at a time, she told herself as she began to marshal the power and the will necessary to compel flesh to obey.

Tomza crouched next to her commander, her fingers finding a jagged shard of stone sticking out of the buckled stair.

"Hold still," she murmured before sawing the sharp stone across her hand. The cut was not as clean as what her flint knife could produce, and she didn't have any of the herbs that would have made this process smoother and safer, but she knew it would work.

And as she was learning, belief would get the job done.

Her blood-smeared hand traced a line from her commander's brow to his chest as her voice rose and fell with words whose meaning she did not know but felt. The power flowed out of her through her opened hand into the blood and then into Torbjorn. More raw and jubilant than it had ever been, her will inhabited his flesh, driving bones back into place and reknitting lacerations deep beneath the skin while herding runnels of blood back to where they belonged. For one glorious instant, she held his life in her red-stained hand. It readily responded to her whims, quickly mended with but a thoughtful intention. Conversely, how easy it would be to—

Tomza lurched back, her smoking, bloody hand coming away

from Torbjorn's chest as she hissed. For a time, she knelt and clutched her trembling, bleeding hand, the only one aware of what had truly transpired. It had been incredible, intoxicating, and dangerous.

In the aftermath of the revelation, everything seemed drained of vibrancy, and even the thrill and rush of terror at their predicament were distant things. She'd nearly given in, and now here she knelt, spent and ashamed, the only one knowing how close it had been.

"Shaper's Fire," Torbjorn gasped beside her. Tomza forced herself to look upon her handiwork. The commander's wounds had not all healed, but the swelling had vanished, and the bruises were mere shadows of the heavy blotches they'd been. When he turned toward her, his movements were free and strong.

"Please," she murmured, fighting to keep from surrendering to the bleak black wave that threatened to overcome her. "Please don't leave Ober behind."

Torbjorn stared into her eyes, and for one awful but freeing moment, she thought he saw the truth there, the naked reality of her near surrender to the power at work through her. In that eternal instant, she didn't know what he might do and even feared it, but it would be an incredible relief not to have to bear the truth alone anymore.

Then he nodded and she saw it was not understanding but assurance that gleamed in his eyes when he set a firm hand on her shoulder.

"No one gets left behind," he promised before drawing himself up and hauling her with him.

"Let's collect the others and see about getting out of here."

They'd found the girl in the cage dangling over the remains of their jailors.

After lowering the cage to the ground, they'd search the mangled leavings for the key to no avail.

"Bloody Ober probably ate it." Waelon grunted as he hefted a gore-slathered axe in both hands. "Along with half of whoever was carrying it."

"Just hurry," Haeda pressed, then addressed the child. "Back of the cage, and cover your face, lass. That's a good girl."

It took three hard strikes to part the lock binding the cage door shut, but with that done, Haeda yanked the door open and was rewarded by the child rushing into her open arms.

"There now," Haeda murmured softly into the blue-streaked tresses of the girl trembling in her embrace. "You're safe. I'm here. It's all right."

Waelon gave a snort as he inspected the axe head for damage before tucking it into his belt.

"Safe's not the word I'd use," the former ranger growled, frowning at the child. "Though I imagine she's the safest of all of us with that light show of hers. Strange that she didn't whip that out when they were stuffing her into that cage."

"Maybe she can't control it," Haeda offered, lifting the child in her arms as she rose to her feet. "Or maybe it only works on demons and the like."

Waelon frowned, but his thoughts were interrupted by a crash behind them. He turned to see that Mabon and Utyrvaul had overturned a large trunk and were spilling its contents on the floor. Amid the mess were some of the items confiscated from the crew upon their capture. Among them were the swords of the two longer-limbed beings. Waelon read the avaricious look in the svartalf's eye as he saw Mabon's family sword tumble free of the mess, but the elf was wise to being observed. With one long finger, he pointed the young man to his sword retrieving his more common blade.

"It's all very fascinating," the elf drawled as he belted on the sword, then scooped up his plated coat. "But I believe we were escaping, not hypothesizing."

"Right you are, Utee," Torbjorn called, mounting the steps followed by an ashen-faced Tomza and a puffing Gromic. "Everyone, snatch up what arms and the like you can. We need to secure passage out of this place."

"Passage?" Utyrvaul asked as he deftly bound the cords of his armor. "That would suggest that we'd be departing this place on something other than our own two feet. Not that I'm complaining, mind you, but last I checked, there was no ferry waiting to bear us to Grayshelf."

"No ferry," Torbjorn agreed as he bent to retrieve a sheathed magsax from under the lower half of its owner. "But when they brought us in, I'm fairly certain I heard worcsvine outside the tower. If they keep those, there is a good chance they'll have a wagon we can drive out of here. I'm surprised that with those exceptionally *sharp* ears, you didn't notice."

Despite their desperate situation, or perhaps because of it, the dwarfs snickered. Waelon guffawed.

"I-I don't get it," Mabon confessed, adjusting his sword on his belt as he looked around the room, bemused.

"Sharp… How droll." The elf sniffed as he tossed his silver hair and looked at the giggling dwarfs archly. "I suppose it isn't worth mentioning that despite our time together, it is still a challenge to discern dwarvish breathing from the snuffling of pigs, so you must excuse my lapse in astuteness."

"All is forgiven," Torbjorn declared, appropriating a shield that hung from a wall mount. "Now, let's get moving before someone else steals our bright idea."

The other dwarfs had found arms and equipment enough among the dead before they set out, and an even greater store when they climbed the steps to a level that must have served as one of the armories for the fortification. While they didn't have time to don full armor since they heard the battle raging outside, they rounded out their collection of shields and found lighter bucklers suited for Mabon and Utyrvaul and stout helmets for all. An intuitive find by Gromic gave them duabuws and several quivers of bolts.

Well-equipped, they ranged up, seeking an exit from the tower that would not deposit them in the courtyard where the transfigured Ober could still be heard raging and slaughtering any that came within reach.

Up and up they climbed, looking for a bridge that connected to the curtain wall, passing the carnage left in Tomza's brother's wake. They tried not to think about what squelched and splattered beneath their boots as they ascended, but it wasn't long before even Waelon was green around the gills. The stink of blood, meat, and spilled guts clung to their clothes, hair, and beards. When at last they came to a rupture in the tower wall through which the cold night air poured, it was a welcome reprieve.

As much to bask in the cleansing air as to assess the situation below, the dwarfs moved to the breach just in time to see the wight lord and his entourage thunder through the gates. None had time to ascertain how the gates had been opened as they watched a score of mounted undead gallop into the bloody courtyard where the ursine terror that was and was not Ober reared in invitation to the new challengers.

The wight lord reined in his steed to circle the massive creature, looking for an angle of approach while his forces rushed to attack it. They leveled their corroded spears as they charged, but the shafts snapped as aged bronze bit humped shoulders and heaving flanks. This only seemed to stoke the roaring fury that descended on lifeless mounts and riders in equal measure.

"I know it's a curse," Waelon remarked as he watched. "But Stones and Bones, I'm glad he's doing the Shaper's own work right now."

Gromic nodded and Haeda sought to cover the girl's face

against the violence when the child stiffened. As in the tunnels when there were ambushed by Ol' Whitey, her body went rigid, and she pointed a finger below. Following the lass' trembling digit, they saw the source of her terror. The wight lord was standing in the stirrups of his cankerous steed, gazing at the girl in Haeda's arms.

Torbjorn saw the hunger in the gleaming eyes within the shadows of its helm and understood they had to move immediately. But where?

His eyes roved about, desperate to find some avenue of escape, and he caught sight of the bridge from the tower to the curtain wall. It was one floor above them, though on it, he spied the backs of dwarvish defenders doggedly beating back the foes assailing the wall. Would they be fortunate enough to escape their notice long enough to circle around and still find the worcsvine in the northern yard? What of the wight?

Torbjorn shook the doubts from his mind and filled his throat with a battle-voiced bark.

"All right, enough gawking. You've all seen a wheezer, so let's get moving before we get to see him any closer."

The flight to the bridge was free of further gore and viscera. Any defenders who had been there had either left to join their brothers in the failing effort on the wall or fled upward in a futile, terrified effort to put space between themselves and the monsters below.

The Bad Badgers rushed onto the narrow bridge of stone unimpeded—to find the waiting wight.

Taller than Utyrvaul and with broad, sweeping shoulders despite his gaunt, desiccated frame, the unliving lord stood upon the bridge. Blade and eyes shone with a ravenous, leeching light.

Behind him, embattled dwarfs strove to fight off the undead clambering up the walls. Those who'd tried to halt the wight had been butchered where they'd stood. These grisly testimonies to the wight's lethal power formed a trail to where the creature blocked the bridge.

The cold, shining eyes of the unliving lord watched them for a moment before he took a single step forward, unhurried and sure.

One hand rose, a blackened, weathered thing beckoning the girl to him.

"Give her to me," the wight commanded in the windy, sighing tone from which the eponymous slur for his kind sprang. "She does not belong to you, but I will have mercy on your ignorance, *tozelchaun*, if you give her to me now."

"I'm under no illusions, wheezer," Torbjorn growled, shield and magsax at the ready. "No matter what, I'll not be giving you anything except steel and iron."

The wight lord cocked his head to one side, his stolen breath whistling through his visor.

"She's not what you think, son of earth," he warned, raising his fell blade over his head. "But if you are determined to die for her like the others, I will oblige you."

"If it saves me having to listen to a blustery dead man, all the better," the dwarvish commander spat, beating the flat of his blade against his shield. "Well, you heard him, shabr'dwans. Our clans are waiting. *BAD BADGERS!*"

The shout was taken up by every living throat on the bridge as bolts flew. Running two abreast, the dwarfs rushed forward.

One bolt was batted aside in a flash of spectral fire by the wight's sword, while another glanced off the curve of his helmet in a shower of sparks. Hoping the wight would be staggered by the impact, Torbjorn and Gromic drove forward to hack the undead's legs out from under him, but the creature was unfazed.

His blade swept down, shattering Torbjorn's shield and burying itself halfway to the boss in Gromic's with a single stroke.

Torbjorn nearly fell off the narrow bridge when he was thrown against the low rail.

Gromic twisted his shield in an attempt to wrench the sword from the wight's grip. The undead gave a wintry laugh as he raised a foot and freed his blade with a kick, sending the stout dwarf stumbling back.

Leaping over Gromic, Waelon rushed forward and hurled his axe at the lifeless warrior. The pilfered, gore-spattered axe spun end over end toward the wight's face, but the blade flashed again and sent the remains of the weapon tumbling away. Waelon had drawn his magsax as he rushed forward, ducking a backswing from the sword to crash forward with a shield bash to the knee and a gutting thrust. The heavy impact to the armored joint knocked the wight back a step, but he twisted away from the stab, allowing the flames on the bronze cuirass to deflect the searching point of the magsax.

Torbjorn righted himself and cast the split shield aside, then sprang forward and hacked at the extended leg of the contorted wight. The stroke felt as though he were hewing at stone rather than once-living tissue, but he'd thrown his weight into it and was rewarded by the knee bowing inward.

A whistling snarl rose from the undead as he swept his sword around, forcing Torbjorn to dive flat to avoid being cleaved in two before he lashed out at Waelon with his free hand. The red-headed dwarf had lunged in for another stab, but the blade bit into the leathery flesh to little effect as the wight's fist crashed into his head. Had it not been for his helmet, the former ranger would have joined his clan then, but the sturdy armor spared him as it was torn from his head with the snapping of its leather chin-strap. Batting at the spots before his eyes, Waelon staggered and found himself stepping back into open air. Gromic's intervention kept him from toppling headfirst to the cobbled courtyard below.

Two more bolts ripped through the air, one punching through bronze to nestle amid the wizened meat of the wight's chest while the other buried itself in the hand reaching toward Gromic's bowed back. The wight ignored the iron barb in its chest, but the bolt through its hand annoyed it by tugging the appendage off-course. The moment was seized upon by Utyrvaul and Mabon, who darted forward, their long blades probing in unison for a line of attack.

The svartalf's superior skill and agility were clear as he feinted with a probing stroke at a knee, only to thrust at the face. The wight leaned into the stab, allowing the blade to slide through his leathery neck before tucking his chin to trap the blade. He swept his sword upward and Utyrvaul sprang back, releasing his hold on his weapon as the undead lord's sword shattered the weapon lodged in its throat.

Mabon, outmatched but determined to put his father's sword to use, pounced and swung with a wild overhead chop. With a contemptuous flick, the wight sought to sunder the young man's sword as he had the elf's, but his blade rebounded from the blow, its edge notched and smoking.

The baleful light within the helm narrowed to piercing slits as he studied Mabon and the sword, the latter glowing ivory.

"Plunder and spoils," the wight lord hissed as he raised his blade to strike Mabon down in a single blow. "That's all you infants care about."

The mighty blow descended, but Mabon's sword swept upward, and with a flash like lightning, the luminous blade sent the undead's weapon tumbling away in seared shards. The young man seemed as stunned by the turn of events as the unliving lord, and they stared at each other for an instant before the wight tilted to one side. Torbjorn clung to his leg, twisting it in his grip.

"Strike, lad!" the commander howled before he was shaken loose by a violent flick of the wight's leg.

Mabon strove to comply, but before the bright blade could

crash down on the scored helm, a bony hand shoved his chest, and he flew back. Arms pinwheeling, he narrowly missed cleaving Utyrvaul's skull to the pointed teeth as he toppled backward. The impact drove the sword from his grip, and it spun end over end as it fell to the courtyard below.

With a snarl, the wight bent and seized Torbjorn by the throat. He hoisted the dwarf off the bridge, and then dangled him, kicking, over open air. The gleaming light within his helmet roiled contemptuously as he looked at the struggling dwarf prying at his iron grip.

He watched his foe squirm like a bug on a pin before opening his hand.

Torbjorn, however, had not let go. He dropped, still holding onto the wight, swinging him toward the bridge's rail. Tucking his legs against his chest, he waited for his boots to meet stone, then he exploded outward, still clutching the wight's arm. The undead might have possessed unholy strength, but surprise and leverage were on the dwarf's side. With a keening shriek, the unliving lord was dragged over the edge with Torbjorn.

Torbjorn managed to get the wight under him just before the courtyard rushed up to meet them.

The dwarf commander felt the impact in his bones. He discovered that while the armored wight had more give than the cobblestones, the difference was negligible. The breath burst out of his lungs, and a shove sent him rolling. Laying on the cobbles, every joint like jelly, Torbjorn watched as the wight rose and hung menacingly over him. The unliving lord tore out the bolt still lodged his hand, then gripped it like a rondel for the coup de grace.

"You made this harder than it had to be," the wight remarked as a huge shadow rose to block the moon.

"You're not the first one to say that to me today, oddly enough." Torbjorn nodded toward the mountain behind the undead. "But right now, you don't need to worry about me."

The wight twisted to see the bear-shaped fury descend upon him, jaws wide. The unliving lord drove the bolt deep into the ursine terror's neck, but like the shattered shafts festooning the monster's shoulders and back, it did nothing to deter his onslaught. Fangs clamped down between shoulder and neck, and the great head of the beast shook and twisted rapidly. Within seconds, the wight was ripped from shoulder to the opposite hipbone, then he separated into two pieces.

The furry manifestation of a storm was not satisfied. Great paws splayed wide, he hurled his weight down on the wight until nothing remained except scraps of bone and metal joined by leathery hanks of gristle.

With a tectonically deep chuff, the beast turned and found that Torbjorn had managed to drag himself to his feet and had scooped up Mabon's sword. The weapon was overlong for a dwarf, but the commander held the blade before him as steadily as he could manage.

"All right, Ober. Easy now," he murmured, trying not to sound as scared as he was. "Just stay calm."

The bared blade seemed to irritate the monster. His lips peeled back from his teeth as his head swung from side to side, sniffing the air, but then his mouth stretched wide, not in a roar but in a yawn. The heavy jaws smacked together twice, then the great dark tongue lolled out, and he puffed out a few steaming breaths before he settled on his haunches, wrath spent.

Like a weary traveler shedding a rain-sodden coat, Ober's body shed the excess mass and all the wounds it had borne, leaving the heads and hafts of the spears that had pierced him to tumble to the cobbles, along with more than a few iron-tipped bolts. Dark fur curled and fell out in clumps. The figure in the courtyard shrank, then resolved into the nude form of Ober.

"Commander?" the young dwarf yawned, his eyes so heavy that he looked ready to pitch forward and take a nap on the cold stone. "What...ooh, what are you doing?"

"Trying to make sure you don't eat me," Torbjorn replied, feeling silly. "Though I suppose now that the danger has passed, I better keep my promise to your sister. Up with you, because promise or no, I don't want to have to carry you about in the buff, danglers floppin' about and all."

CHAPTER TWENTY-SIX

"Come here, you damned pigs!"

The voice coming from the worcsvine's pen was familiar to Torbjorn.

While the last of his dwans fought off the crumbling forces of the fallen wight lord, Tweldwan Jozef of Merihn was in front of the pens in the north yard, trying desperately to harness a team of swine to a wagon that stood near a postern gate that was just wide enough to accommodate the vehicle. The pigs, having heard the raucous battle and scented the musk of predators of all stripes, were in no mood to acquiesce, and they also seemed keen to stay away from the courtyard.

A recalcitrant sow managed to twist free of the Tweldwan's grip and kick out with her sharp hooves, catching the officer a glancing blow to the shins. Jozef was still staggering about, swearing and puffing, when the Bad Badgers came upon him, weapons drawn and faces hard.

"Oh, kak," the dwarf groaned, his eyes darting around for a source of help. He found none.

"You can go ahead and squeal," Waelon offered as he stalked

forward, sword in hand. "I'd love to see how you'd explain abandoning your post to go play with the pigs."

The tweldwan lurched away from the fiery dwarf with the bare blade but found that he was hemmed in on all sides.

"Please," he squeaked, scrambling back, only to find himself pinned against the side of the wagon. "There's no reason we can't escape the slaughter together. I mean, that's all I wanted."

Torbjorn stepped forward, one arm around Ober's bare back while the other held the magsax he'd traded Mabon's family's sword for. The point hovered in front of the cowardly dwarf's nose for a moment, then Torbjorn lowered the blade with a grim smile.

"Slaughter?" he asked, raising a bushy eyebrow quizzically. "Don't you mean 'victory?' The day is yours, Tweldwan!"

Jozef blinked rapidly, then looked around at the ring of faces, searching for a clue as to the joke.

"I-I... I don't understand," the castellan stuttered, turning at last to Torbjorn. "The wight... His army, they... They're..."

"Oh, I apologize! You missed a few things while you were trying to hitch up your wagon," Torbjorn told him, only a hint of a growl in his voice. "The wight lord's in pieces—truly a historic moment—and like puppets with cut strings, the clackers are just hanging about. The auxiliaries are being chased off right now, but without the wight to keep them in line, they'll be lucky to make it home without turning on each other. That about wraps things up, don't you think?"

Utyrvaul cleared his throat with a dainty cough before adding, "To be fair, I'm sure there are some gremalkins creeping around, looking for whatever fodder they can still snag. Nasty buggers think with their stomachs."

Torbjorn cocked an eyebrow but nodded as he turned back to the cowering tweldwan. "I suppose that's true. If you hurry, you might be able to lead the hunt for the beasts. Who knows? That might even make your dwans forget the fact that you were nowhere to be found when the attack came."

Again, Jozef looked around the ring of unflinching gazes and waited for the trap to be sprung, but he was met by more silence and stares.

"S-s-so, you'll let me go, just like that?"

Torbjorn, with Ober in tow, stepped back to clear the way for the castellan.

"All I've wanted since we met is to do my duty," the commander replied, his voice growing steelier with each word. "I suggest you go and do yours."

It took Tweldwan Jozef of Merihn a few moments to work up the courage to take that first step between the Bad Badgers, but after the first foot fell, the other hastily followed. After he was clear of their icy glares, he didn't bother to look back, which was a mistake since dark shapes detached from the shadows of the yard to follow him.

Torbjorn's crew had other matters to attend to.

"It… It can't be!" Haeda gasped as she squinted at the nearest worcsvine snuffling about the yard in the gloom. "Do you realize who these are?"

"What are you on about?" Torbjorn asked a heartbeat before a piercing yowl rose from the direction Jozef had departed. Other less indistinguishable but no less unpleasant sounds followed. Those in the yard did their best to ignore them, including the pigs, who continued their mumbling grunts as they nosed about the hard earth.

"They're my team!" Haeda crowed, doing a little dance with the girl, who happily joined despite being bumfuzzled as to why. "Hohoho, my girls made it all the way back! Never doubted them for a second, not *my* team!"

Incredulous frowns graced every dwarven face at the driver's declaration.

"You mean, these are the pigs you turned loose back at the

Teeth?" Gromic inquired doubtfully. "How do you know they're the same ones?"

Haeda ceased dancing, provoking a frown from the girl. She turned it on Gromic, following her caregiver's example.

"You don't think I know my own team?"

Gromic's eyes widened when he realized the severity of the mistake he'd just made. Not daring to move or speak, he allowed his eyes to plead with the dwarfs around him.

"I think what tub-o'-guts means is, isn't it more likely that these are just some sows that look like your team, and you're letting wishful thinking cloud your judgment?" Waelon offered as graciously as he could.

"These are *my* girls," Haeda replied in a tone that brooked no argument, then turned her back on the doubtful glances of her peers. "I'll bloody well prove it."

Haeda gave a single short trilling whistle, followed by a few clicks of her tongue.

At the call, eight sleek sows detached themselves from the milling herd and trotted to the nearby wagon. There were a few uncertain grunts and snuffles, as one would expect for creatures a few weeks out of practice, but a moment later, all eight stood at the ready, snouts raised to accommodate the harness being slipped over their heads.

Haeda turned smartly about, hands on her hips, to fix her colleagues with a look of smug satisfaction. Her posture was adopted by the child at her side.

"Never doubted you or the girls for a second, Haeda," Torbjorn lied as he dragged the drooping Ober to the wagon bed. He turned to the others with a bark in his voice. "Well, what are you waiting for? Gromic, Waelon! Get that postern open while Haeda rigs up the team and the rest of you get loaded! Oh, and someone fetch a blanket from that stall over there. Ober can't ride all the way to Grayshelf naked, though it'd be funny to see him try."

Without further prompting, Utyrvaul sprang over to the

aforementioned stall and hurried back with the bristle-flecked blanket held gingerly in front of him.

"I hope being willing to touch this shows how little I appreciate dwarvish ideas of entertainment."

The dwarfs chuckled at the elf's puckered expression as Haeda's team drew the wagon through the postern gate.

They passed into the night, still laughing.

AUTHOR NOTES - AARON D. SCHNEIDER

WRITTEN AUGUST 3, 2022

Dear Reader,

Well, out of the frying pan and into the fire, eh?

We've got a long way to go yet with our stout compatriots and their ever-growing entourage of miscreants and secrets. Things in the Ysgand Vale are going to get pretty interesting, so I'd advise you not to stray too far. We wouldn't want you losing track of things and have to start the adventure all over just to keep things straight, now, would we?

Speaking of keeping things straight, I have been having a time (as well as the time of my life) keeping everything in line as I continue to work on the *Dwarvish Dirty Dozen*, along with a few other projects, which should hopefully come out this fall. That is one of the great things and one of the hard things (in the possible sense) about working with the great folks at LMBPN, and that is the incredible potential to tell the stories a madman like me wants to tell with the support of phenomenal people who want to see me succeed.

From teams that work in editing, covers, reader feedback, marketing, and I'm sure things I've never even thought of, they are a fantastic conglomeration of motley crews all skippered under the madcap captain himself, Michael Anderle (duly partnered with his lovely bride Judith), who keeps our ship upright and headed for that horizon.

Truly, dear Reader, they aren't perfect, but they've been good to me and to so many others. I don't feel I give them enough credit most of the time.

But when you have such lovely people to work with, it stings that much more when you have to say goodbye to one of them.

Not long before I finished this book, the lovely woman who edited the *Outcast Royal* series and worked with me on several other projects over the past year sadly passed away. I won't pretend that she and I were the closest of friends, but working on creative endeavors like this, especially an author and editor, requires trust and a vulnerability that might be hard to understand for someone who's never gone through the process. This person takes something you've poured yourself into, and you have to believe that they want good for you, and yes, some of that good comes from them being painfully honest, but it's to make you better, clearer, and wiser.

She was that sort of woman—one who would give it to you straight even if it was hard or it hurt, not because she didn't care, but because she *did*, and that was how she knew you could hear her, then grow and improve. The world is poorer for her passing on that score alone and more besides.

Perhaps that is how I should end this little love note between you and me, with an exhortation to be honest. There have always been lies in this world (something about a forked tongue and some fruit), and there have always been those who are more in love with lies than they are with the truth. If we are all honest, oftentimes, we've been those people, but we don't have to be. Not today, and not tomorrow. Choose truth, choose to seek it, to know it, to share it, and most importantly, choose not to fear it.

I once read in the most important book something like,
"Then you will know the truth, and the truth shall set you free."

Sincere Regards,
Aaron D. Schneider

AUTHOR NOTES - MICHAEL ANDERLE

AUGUST 3, 2022

Thank you for not only reading this story with these author notes as well.

DWARVES, DWARVES and MORE DWARVES.

Ignoring politics for just a moment.

I graduated high school in 1986, and fiction related to fantasy works held a renaissance in the late 70s, and early 80s after the success (or continued success) of J.R.R. Tolkien's Lord of the Rings and Dungeons & Dragons from TSR lit a fire in fiction.

So, I got in on some of the best new work when the genre exploded a second time during my formative years of reading.

I have always wondered whether Tolkien and others used some of the different people around the world as "suggestions" for some of the nonhuman races in the fantasy genre.new paragraph

For example, let's take a hardheaded, obstinate, hard-drinking, ready-to-fight group of individuals and call them dwarves.

Out of the many different peoples populating the world (and I know you can think of two or three different groups to the description above), I have always thought *Russians* were the closest group of people that we might consider dwarves that are out there.

Think about it, grumpy, hard-drinking describes a Russian, as well as a party animal, boisterous and drinking. Except for the vodka vs. beer part.

That part is obviously Germans.

Since I see most of my Russian stories filtered through American media, I could be way off base about all of this. For all I know, the American media and news outlets have glossed over enough positive details of the Russian people to make my "dwarves came from Russians" concept totally bogus.

Before those of you with blood from Ireland or Scotland get on my case, I tend to think of you guys as Barbarians.

It fits, right?

If you want to take this example a little farther, I often attribute elves to either Japanese or the Chinese (physically more Japanese, I think. Tall and thin?) However, having visited China a couple of times, I think a case could be made for the Chinese as well.

The more I learn about people from around the world, the more I see how Tolkien was influenced by history and how people have been represented in their own literature and the literature he must have read.

Do you have your own theories or know what information influenced Tolkien? If so, feel free to jot your notes in a review of the book and let me know!

I look forward to talking to you again in the next story.

Ad Aeternitatem,

Michael Anderle

I have a couple of short stories you can read that I am sharing from my STORIES with Michael Anderle newsletter here:

AUTHOR NOTES - MICHAEL ANDERLE

https://michael.beehiiv.com/

CONNECT WITH THE AUTHORS

Connect with Aaron Schneider

Website:
https://www.aarondschneider.com/

Email List:
https://www.aarondschneider.com/free-short-story-download-the-tops-tails-of-dreams/

Facebook:
https://www.facebook.com/authoraarondschneider/

Amazon:
https://www.amazon.com/Aaron-D-Schneider/e/B07H8WZ2HT/

Connect with Michael Anderle and sign up for his email list here:

Website: http://lmbpn.com

Email List: http://lmbpn.com/email/

https://www.facebook.com/LMBPNPublishing

https://twitter.com/MichaelAnderle

https://www.instagram.com/lmbpn_publishing/

https://www.bookbub.com/authors/michael-anderle

OTHER BOOKS BY AARON D. SCHNEIDER

The Warring Realm Series

War-Born

War-Torn

War-Sworn

Rings of the Inconquo

(with A.L. Knorr)

Born of Metal (Book 1)

Metal Guardian (Book 2)

Metal Angel (Book 3)

World's First Wizard

(with Michael Anderle)

Witchmarked (Book 1)

Sorcerybound (Book 2)

Wizardborn (Book 3)

The Outcast Royal Series

(with Michael Anderle)

Circle In The Deep (Book 1)

Voice On The Wind (Book 2)

Doom Under The Shadow (Book 3)

Join Aaron's Email List

https://www.aarondschneider.com/free-short-story-download-the-tops-tails-of-dreams/

BOOKS BY MICHAEL ANDERLE

Sign up for the LMBPN email list to be notified of new releases and special deals!

https://lmbpn.com/email/

For a complete list of books by Michael Anderle, please visit:

www.lmbpn.com/ma-books/

www.ingramcontent.com/pod-product-compliance
Lightning Source LLC
LaVergne TN
LVHW041800060526
838201LV00046B/1064